From Across the Room

From Across the Room

Gina L. Mulligan

FIVE STAR
A part of Gale, Cengage Learning

Farmington Hills, Mich • San Francisco • New York • Waterville, Maine
Meriden, Conn • Mason, Ohio • Chicago

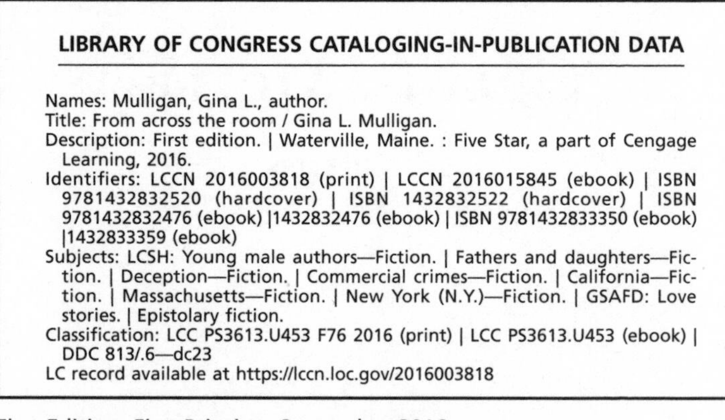
LIBRARY OF CONGRESS CATALOGING-IN-PUBLICATION DATA

Names: Mulligan, Gina L., author.
Title: From across the room / Gina L. Mulligan.
Description: First edition. | Waterville, Maine. : Five Star, a part of Cengage Learning, 2016.
Identifiers: LCCN 2016003818 (print) | LCCN 2016015845 (ebook) | ISBN 9781432832520 (hardcover) | ISBN 1432832522 (hardcover) | ISBN 9781432832476 (ebook) |1432832476 (ebook) | ISBN 9781432833350 (ebook) |1432833359 (ebook)
Subjects: LCSH: Young male authors—Fiction. | Fathers and daughters—Fiction. | Deception—Fiction. | Commercial crimes—Fiction. | California—Fiction. | Massachusetts—Fiction. | New York (N.Y.)—Fiction. | GSAFD: Love stories. | Epistolary fiction.
Classification: LCC PS3613.U453 F76 2016 (print) | LCC PS3613.U453 (ebook) | DDC 813/.6—dc23
LC record available at https://lccn.loc.gov/2016003818

First Edition. First Printing: September 2016
Find us on Facebook– https://www.facebook.com/FiveStarCengage
Visit our website– http://www.gale.cengage.com/fivestar/
Contact Five Star™ Publishing at FiveStar@cengage.com

Printed in the United States of America
1 2 3 4 5 6 7 20 19 18 17 16

This book inspired me to start Girls Love Mail, a charity that gives handwritten letters of encouragement to women newly diagnosed with breast cancer. *From Across the Room* is dedicated to every letter recipient, writer, volunteer, health professional, and breast cancer organization who supports Girls Love Mail and gives this novel more meaning than I ever expected. Together we can encourage the world, one handwritten letter at a time.

For more information about Girls Love Mail, visit www.GirlsLoveMail.com.

AUTHOR'S NOTE

Letters are gifts with the power to heal, charm, entertain, and even persuade. They are historical records and sacred mementos. In a society dominated by text messages and emails, the lost art of letter writing provides a unique and voyeuristic escape. Run your fingers over the fine linen, imagine the delicate script, and let the letters transport you to a time when every word required careful consideration and a person's true character remained forever safe inside the folds.

Prologue

From the Desk of Henry James– October 21, 1881

To write well you must understand we all work in the dark. Doubt may either fuel your enthusiasm or block your way, but true passion is not something you can turn on and off. As a doctor listens to a heartbeat not with his ears but his soul, for you to become a writer you must live within your work. Think of each pen stroke as the advancement of your cause and do not waste paper on merely cataloging facts. Explore, relish, surprise, and delight in the words so someday your readers can do the same. The novelist faces many unknowns, so remember this—the novel exists to represent life.

SUMMER 1888

June 6, 1888.

DEAR AVERY—

In another age my kind was near extinction, killed in battle while struggling to put on chainmail. Today a writer can travel to a seaside resort, slouch on a padded lounge, and appraise your furious letter in comfort. Rest assured I am toiling away on the book, but as a matter of principle, I must refute your accusation I am again irresponsible. *Again?* You know my pages were delayed last time due to a simple miscalculation. According to my lunar calendar, I was a month early. Nevertheless, this time my delay in sending the promised chapters was unavoidable and shows a depth of character you might also find hard to believe.

Are you at least curious why I journeyed all the way to the Hotel Del Coronado to find my muse? A hotel is the ideal setting. The onslaught of fresh arrivals provides constant fodder while the locale ensures variety. True, high season calls for stamina; writing requires such keen skills of observation. Though some are born with this gift, the rest of us must learn the nuances of peering and loitering while enduring the occasional knock on the head with a beaded evening bag. You see what I must suffer for your greatness and the publisher's profits?

Before you fling your spectacles and run your thick fingers through your thin hair, I am not in the least trying to be flippant. I am well aware that, as my agent, your income is based on my hard work, and losing Harper & Brothers Publishing is a distasteful consequence we both wish to avoid. My career is dependent on the publisher and their dotted line so let me explain my tardiness with enough background and detail to appease, nay impress, our good friends at Harper's.

Though the hotel offers many diversions, I abstained from the temptation of billiards and chess and set out my writing supplies even before unpacking. You see, Avery, right to work. Looking for inspiration, I even arranged a city tour. After a turn through the respectable streets of San Diego, a few extra coins persuaded my hackney driver to take me to the Stingaree District. In contrast to the luxury of the hotel, this area is described only in whispers and my intent was a quick survey to jot down scenery notes.

San Diego was built around the Mission Basilica and remnants of Spanish settlements. Along with drab wooden storefronts, much of the city proper is laden with handmade signs advertising clean office space and cheap irrigation supplies. It seems San Diego has stalled for need of water and respectable industry. Of course men always find ways to occupy their time. I just wonder what Father Serra would think if he saw what goes on just around the corner from his mission.

Trainloads of high-flying men in shirtsleeves blanketed walkways lit more by cigars than the dirty lamps, and powdered chippies in purple corsets were draped over balconies like flags on Decoration Day. I stepped over men gambling and passing jugs of Tarantula Juice right on the street corners, then a pitch-man with a greasy complexion slapped a pot of milky cream in my hand and said, "For the French Pox." Before I could react, a harlot with ruby cheeks and a vacant stare offered me a way to need the jar of ointment.

Unrecognizable music blared from every direction, and my disgust at the scene was almost bested by the smell. The stench from the chickens, horses, and opium dens (their curtains parted to calloused deputies) was so thick not even the sea breeze could carry it away.

The district is small, so with the end in sight, I turned to go back, when all of sudden I was shoved and fell right into a stack of hay. The landing was soft but my surprise meant I also got a literal taste of the area. As I spit out sprigs and brushed bits from my waistcoat, I spotted my assailant: a woman running down the walkway with fistfuls of her skirt hiked up to her knees. She was chasing a man.

In truth, what caught my attention was the lady's bloomers. Shenanigans are expected in such an area, but I could tell by the pastel brocade lace that the owner was not one of the regulars. I watched as the woman pursued the fleeing man around a corner. When I then heard her scream, I sprung into action like a mother cheetah.

To avoid the crowded walkway, I darted around a hitching post and hurled myself into the street. Just as my feet hit the dirt, a chuck wagon swerved and I scrambled back into my haystack. Ignoring the driver's profanity, I regained my balance and charged down the center of the road, leaving a feed trail.

My pulse quickened until I no longer heard the awful music. As I ran toward the scream, my jacket caught on a piece of wood jutting from one of the buildings. I spun with the grace of a discus Olympian and slipped free in one fluid motion. A few more steps and I rounded the corner. My pounding heart seized as I skidded to a stop.

The woman stood ten feet down the dim alley with her

hands raised over her head. Her back was to me, but at the sound of my entrance she turned to glance over her shoulder. I smiled. It was her.

The young lady and I, shall we say, met at the hotel's newcomers gala. If repeated I shall deny this account, but because I respect your usual good humor I admit colliding into the stunned woman while examining the ballroom's ceiling. The Crown Room is topped with a marvelous hand-fitted arch made of imported sugar pine, and I was captivated by the elaborate carvings. The young lady, however, was startled and I was indeed thankful for my tanned cheeks. After apologies I hoped she would consider a dance, but she slipped into the crowd before I could ask. You can imagine my surprise to find myself staring at her across a foul alleyway.

She fixed her eyes on mine. "This young man," she said, nodding toward her assailant, her arms still raised over her head, "was just telling me that his sister is very ill and he needs money for medicine." Then she addressed the young man. "You said your name is George, isn't that right?" He gave a slight nod. "Well, I'm sorry, George, there's no money in my handbag." Her voice was refined and tranquil. If not for the sound of scurrying rodents and the smell of trash, she might have been at a society luncheon.

My eyes adjusted, and I saw George was a slight boy of no more than fifteen. A pistol quivered in his hand and sweat trickled along his hairline.

The lad was scared, not stupid. If the handbag was empty, he wanted to know why she had chased him. I too wanted an answer to that question, but when he snarled and waved the gun I chimed in, "Ladies are very particular about their handbags. She likely has a container of rouge she can't part with."

The woman ignored my comment and explained she always carried a special hair comb from her sister and hated to lose it. "It's not worth anything but has great sentimental value. When I was a little girl, my sister and I would look through our mother's dressing table while she was out. We tried on her hair pins and gloves and pretended we were debutantes. Well, one night . . ."

George was mesmerized. As she continued with her story I inched toward the pistol.

I found the woman's voice inviting so I risked sneaking a glance at her. She was dressed for a daytime outing in a starched white ruffled shirt over a full navy skirt. A thick belt accented her narrow waist and her chestnut hair was piled under a curved-brimmed hat she wore tilted forward.

"So I understand not wanting to lose someone you love, George. Please let us help you," she ended.

His arm went slack. I surged forward, grabbed the muzzle of the gun, and pulled it from his hand. Tears slid down the boy's cheeks as he took what I offered from my billfold then returned the stolen handbag. Before we could ask any more questions, he rushed from the alley with his head lowered.

Expecting the delicate beauty to swoon and collapse in my arms, I steadied myself. Instead she turned to me with her hands planted on her hips and said, "*Rouge?* You think a woman would chase a bandit for a tin of rouge?"

In my shock I stammered, "I . . . don't know. I . . . didn't think a woman would chase a bandit."

She raised her hand to cover a devious smile. "I'm not sure why I did it. There isn't any money in there, or a hair comb for that matter. It was just instinct."

Though a bit stunned and more than a bit intrigued, I

removed my Derby. "Thomas Gadwell. It's very nice to meet you."

She curtsied as if we were back at the grand ballroom. "I'm Mary Harting," she said. "It's a pleasure to match a name with the shoe print on my gown." When I began to apologize again, she waved her hands and tilted her head back so I could see her light-blue eyes under the slant of her hat. She accented the playfulness in her voice with a wide grin. "I believe now we're even, though you were right in the middle of the walkway when I nudged you."

"And you had a bandit to catch. I completely understand."

We chuckled until shouting from the street drew our attention and we decided it safer to relocate. Before escorting Miss Harting from the scene, I unloaded the pistol, slid the gun into my overcoat pocket, and threw the bullets down the alley. As we emerged, I realized no one had responded to her scream. The gambling and frolic continued as if nothing had happened. I also noticed my companion was still grinning.

She accepted my arm as we made our way among blustering drunks and "steerers" paid to lure patrons. Miss Harting tried to stroll with an air of ease but soon she was like a sightseer at the zoo. She stopped in front of an overfilled chophouse and gaped at men using shards of broken glass as darts. When a fiddler passed by, plucking two strings and belting a song heard only in public baths, her eyes followed him until she turned in a full circle.

"It's like something in a dime novel. I thought everyone was exaggerating," she said.

"Unfortunately . . ." I let the sentiment speak for itself and asked the question pressing at my lips.

She explained a simple curiosity about the area and saw

no impropriety in a short visit, especially since her parents were occupied for the evening. And, she said, if gentlemen, such as me, were allowed to travel unaccompanied she felt it fair to be granted the same privilege. "Do you agree, Mr. Gadwell?" She peered at me with raised eyebrows. "Or are you among those who believe women faint from reading newspaper headlines and medical journals."

I laughed. "I thought dashing young men caused women to faint."

"I'll let you in on a little secret, Mr. Gadwell. Fainting is a great way to escape dashing young men." She had a relaxed, genuine manner I found refreshing.

"So, Miss Harting," I began, when I made the connection. "Harting? As in the railroad?"

Her shoulders tensed but she spoke with refined gentleness as she admitted her father was Charlton Harting of Harting Railways. "I'm sure you've heard the rumors about his temper. Lies and gross exaggerations. My father's been a bit irritable this trip, but normally he's wonderful and caring."

A chill ran down my spine. As you know, not all of the rumors about Charlton Harting are about his temper.

I wanted to change the subject when a thought left me numb. "What would your father say if he knew you were here?"

"My father," she mumbled.

"Yes, your father. I can only imagine—"

"No, my father . . ." Miss Harting pointed to a round man in a velvet-trimmed frock coat and top hat. He was charging toward us on the other side of the street, the tails of his coat flapping in his own wake.

Miss Harting froze so I seized her hand and pulled her through an open doorway. The sound of clanging bottles and a tuneless piano filled my ears and I knew where we were even before she whispered, “Unbelievable.”

The hot saloon smelled of sour ale and unshaven men. Our entrance met with a few raised heads, but the men seemed more interested in their drinks. We dashed across the tavern to the table farthest from the door and sunk into chairs tucked in the shadowed corner.

“What in the world is my father doing here? He doesn’t frequent places like this.” She paused then asked, “Does he?”

I was about to offer my ignorance when Mr. Harting stepped into the saloon. Miss Harting gasped.

Mr. Harting marched to a table near the bar and sat across from a man in a straw boater and a russet knee-length cloak. They exchanged a brief greeting before Mr. Harting pulled an envelope from his jacket and set it in the center of the table. A waiter approached but Mr. Harting waved him away without a glance. The men sat staring at each other. Even from our distance the intensity made me uncomfortable.

At last the man in the cloak reached for the envelope, looked inside, and then nodded before sliding the envelope into a satchel beside him on the floor. Both men rose and the stranger held out his hand. Instead of a handshake, Mr. Harting lunged forward, grabbed the man’s collar and yanked him across the table until his face was but inches from his own. Sweat beaded at each man’s temple, but only Mr. Harting’s brow twitched with anger.

We were too far away to hear anything, but it was obvious whatever was said was most vital. The man’s straw hat wobbled like a stereoscope viewer until Mr. Harting released him with a shove and the man fell backward. To his credit, the stranger adjusted his lapel before retaking his seat. Mr. Harting straightened his own jacket and appeared ready to leave when he paused and turned in our direction.

My companion pressed against the wall and clenched her fingers as if to pray. This is not to say I stayed relaxed. A whiskey might have helped. Whatever caught his attention was fleeting, and Mr. Harting left without looking back.

Wanting to sound gallant, I assured her we were not seen. As she slumped forward on the table, the other man stood up, swung the satchel on his arm, and left. Miss Harting agreed to my suggestion we get back to the hotel; however, she wanted to know if I recognized the man. I did not, but suggested he looked like a business acquaintance.

"I don't think so. Father's workmen are thick from years of swinging spike drivers, and the desk men are usually scrawny. My father likes to be the biggest one in the office. He says small men are easier to control."

There was no time for a response even if I had one. Three dancing girls emerged from behind a crimson velvet curtain. I scrambled to my feet to block Miss Harting's view then offered her my arm. As we moved to leave, however, a tall chap in a dark overcoat stepped in front of us. For a moment I thought Mr. Harting had indeed spotted us. I straightened. Then I saw the rifle.

"Seems like you two have lost your way."

I reached for the gun in my pocket, but Miss Harting put her hand on my arm. "Thank you, Sheriff, we were just leaving."

I sighed when I saw his badge. The sheriff tipped his hat to the lady. As I passed he growled, "You're a lucky ninny."

"You have no idea," I replied. I pulled out the pistol by

the muzzle and dropped it on the table.

After checking the street for fathers, we found our way out of the quarter and hailed a coach. We were silent, though qualms over what a powerful man would hand-deliver in a tawdry saloon bobbled around us in the rocking carriage. To change the mood, I praised her bravery and compassion. She again surprised me.

"I've seen desperate conditions, Mr. Gadwell, I assure you. And I've witnessed my share of injustice and cruelty. But tonight, the lust and greed, it was somehow more tragic. Why do we bother with the appearances of morality? Why all the bowing and draping shawls over our shoulders in the horrible heat when men behave like that? I understand poverty. I know why people like George are forced into bad situations, but most of those men tonight were wealthy gentlemen. Did you notice all the gold studs? My father was even carrying his diamond pocket watch."

Under difference circumstances the ride might have been a bit romantic; her petite shoulder just touching mine. Instead my thoughts were on the enormity of sitting beside the daughter of Charlton Harting.

When we reached the hotel, I escorted my damsel in distress through the quiet lobby to the main staircase. She thanked me for an unforgettable evening and repaid my bravery by allowing me to call her Mary. Then she leaned forward and whispered in my ear, "By the by, I saw the dancing girls." She winked and disappeared up the staircase leaving me with my mouth flopped open.

So you see, Avery, I was called to arms. What else could be done? Harper & Brothers will understand chivalry must be proven, and it may be argued such acts are the linchpin to a good story. Needless to say, once this letter is sealed I shall fill my inkwell and get back to work. Unlike the time

I had a hankering for pickled turnips and wound up trapped in the root cellar, nothing will keep me from finishing this book. Of course, you must concede that after such an ordeal, Miss Harting shall need some measure of soothing. But how long can that take.

Your humble servant,
Thomas

June 7, 1888.

DEAR MOTHER—

I received your telegram. No, I was not shanghaied through a trap door at The Beantown Tavern. My escape from summer in Boston was perhaps impulsive, but you can assure Aunt Ruth the hotel is not overcrowded with men in jockey hats brandishing Spencer rifles and fishing lures. She may cancel her trip.

Having received the recommendation for this California jaunt from Henry (you know him as Mr. James), I imagined a maudlin inn promoting fireside confessions and pithy dining selections like Hawthorne Hasty Pudding. Surprises began the moment I arrived.

Ten miles of lurching turns had soured my exhilaration, not to mention my stomach, when at last the train gave its final sigh. We arrived at dusk, and through my window I saw golden strands of light shimmering on the Pacific. Though the smell of the crisp air was stirring and I was eager to part from the jarring iron horse, my fellow riders were quite preoccupied.

Gentlemen threatened a frenzied list of litigation if monogrammed trunks were damaged. The ladies, fretful about sand in their boots, tightened their mantles against the breeze and sent husbands to fetch fleeing bonnets. There was also consternation over costumes for a masquerade ball and how the damp climate flattens ruffles. In truth, I was discouraged by their nonchalant reaction to the splendid welcome.

Colorful streamers waved like banderoles at the Boston Harbor Festival and a brass band played "Liberty Bell Quickstep" from somewhere in the depths of the hotel. Stewards in emerald waistcoats and black bowties weaved through the crowd with trays of champagne, and a man in a white tailcoat announced dinner was served in the dining room at eight o'clock. Toasting my arrival to the West with champagne felt as awkward as the first time Father handed me the reins. I expected a glass of watered ale in a dirty tin cup. In fact, my thoughts were on such a barley pop when a porter in a red Kepi cap tapped my shoulder and took my satchel.

"Welcome, my good sir, to San Diego's new Hotel Del Coronado. On behalf of the staff I'd like to extend our deepest appreciation for your patronage. A complimentary bottle of Chateau Margaux is in your suite, and we'd like to offer you a hansom cab tour of the city. Your attendant can arrange your visit whenever you're interested and available.

"I mention available, sir, because here at The Del there are many ways to occupy yourself. Each morning you'll receive a list of the day's activities and the appropriate attire for the evening's entertainment. In addition to your personal attendant, there's a concierge to arrange equipment rental for archery, croquet, golf, and boating. Our kitchen is equipped to handle any dietary restrictions, and the smoking lounge is well stocked. Our only goal is to provide you with a memorable summer, sir. We're proud to serve you in any way possible."

His lavish greeting paled in comparison to the lady behind him.

Before me was a generous Queen Anne painted stark white. Long shadows caressed her red dome roof, and I saw the fetching silhouette of grand turrets, carved spindles, and a large walking deck leading to the sea. Rows of spacious windows faced the ocean like soldiers ready to march, and an ethereal mist swirled across the veranda.

"Lovely," I muttered.

"Why, thank you, young man. It's new. Bought it especially for the trip."

Mother, I turned to see a round woman adjusting a hat with black feathers and gold ladybugs swinging from brass wire. It reminded me of a child's mobile. As she walked away I heard her call out, "You see, Stella, I told you bugs were fashionable this year."

A second announcement for dinner inspired the newcomers, so I followed my comrades across the threshold. It was almost as if I had never left Boston.

The intimate lobby was a flurry of excitement. Patent leather heels and boisterous chatter echoed on the marble floor as receptionists matched visitors with their attendants. Settled guests, their pressed jackets and tanned skin worn as a coveted prize, weaved through the fresh faces. Their inspection was thorough.

A lady's nod or a gent's familiar handshake meant an invitation to dinner and a front row seat for the chamber orchestra. You, of course, know I sought neither. Instead I found a restful spot near the concierge desk, propped myself against the mahogany paneling, and took up my usual role. I admit with pleasure what first drew my attention.

Two pleasing young ladies were well positioned on an embroidered loveseat. Their silk fans fluttered with excited agitation as they surveyed the crowd and whispered in each other's ears. The ladies looked refreshed in long, white linen dresses with large straw hats. As I wiped bits of coal from my Chesterfield, I was amused by the skill with which they tilted their broad brims to camouflage their stares. You need not worry, I turned away before I caught their eyes and continued my observation.

Caramel light from the gas lamps softened the society.

French doors were opened to the rush of the waves and the evening's meal promised a healthy portion of garlic. However, not until my eyes drifted to the far side of the lobby was I quite in awe.

Do you remember the gold birdcage in that Parisian boutique? Beside a group of men pulling calling cards from their vest pockets was a hydraulic elevator that looked just like that elaborate coop. Through the open slats guests waved as they rode to the upper floors. It was a marvel to see their feet lift right off the ground. Alas, my enjoyment at watching the elevator was interrupted.

The girls on the loveseat rose and linked arms. They ambled toward me with their fans resting at their sides and stopped at the concierge desk.

"We've forgotten our table assignment. Please look up Adams, Elizabeth and Emily."

The girls smiled at me then turned away to speak in low voices. Just then a lithe man with a sharp chin and deep wrinkles approached and asked, "Mr. Thomas M. Gadwell?" My attendant, Walter, led me to the elevator but not before I tipped my bowler and left the young ladies giggling.

My ferry to the second floor was thrilling, and I, too, felt compelled to wave to strangers in the lobby. Then Walter showed me down a spacious hallway to the last suite. Though I suffer in many ways for my craft, I freely admit accommodation is not one of them.

The room is spacious with a sitting area and comfortable feather bed. There is a private privy and a thoughtful balcony providing marvelous views. The curved coastline stretches for miles in both directions with jagged cliffs hovering in the distance, and beyond the hotel's landscaped gardens are secluded pockets of stiff sea grass you might feel compelled to weed.

Still, if you reconsider a trip, the hotel's craftsmanship and intriguing company are worth the arduous journey from Boston. Provided, of course, you forbid father to bring his newspapers aboard the train. Not even you could withstand seven days trapped with father and his convictions.

I must take my leave, as I have an engagement for afternoon tea and a quartet is playing this evening. Please tell Father I hope he recovers from his lingering cold, and enjoy your tulip garden before you leave for your vacation in Newport. Lest you fear I shall be stirred by the wild frontier to grow a thick mustache and long side whiskers, I assure you that the society is conventional, management forbids saloon gunfights, and I have yet to meet a rowdy gold prospector—of course I hope to soon.

Your loving son,
Thomas

June 10, 1888.

DEAR MISS MARY HARTING—

Thank you again for a charming afternoon. I feared nothing could surpass the excitement of our escapade, but then I never suspected your interest in sharp arrows.

Even with such delicate, feminine hands you had a steady aim and did a fine job of breaking in the new target. You also had the appropriate archer's look of concentration. Based on your snickering, I imagine my grimace resembled eating sour candy. But I again remind you it was my shot that provided our fresh quail for lunch. That the instructor had to dive for safety was part of my skill.

If your bravery has not waned, I hope you will join me tomorrow so I may again flaunt my talent with a teacup. As the manager has banned me from picking up another bow while on hotel grounds, perhaps we can explore other interests. I hear the bicycle trails are comfortably wide, as are the bicycle seats.

Respectfully,
Thomas Marcus Gadwell

June 13, 1888.

DEAR MARY—

As we sat together on the hotel's impressive veranda I longed to stand upon the chaise and proclaim my true feelings. Is such frankness too presumptuous for our new acquaintance? Conformity be dashed, I must tell you.

I despise lemonade. It tastes like spoiled wine mixed with bits of twine. I confess because I fear you may have misinterpreted my distasteful expression as you spoke of women's suffrage. On the contrary, you have given me a new perspective.

Your argument for equality was well organized and quite passionate. Few women in polite society share their frustration for a lifetime of quiet reflection, and I understand why you are sometimes bored with needlepoint and summer parties. Your candor is stimulating—as is your astute discretion.

We live in a culture where women in need of employment are forced into factory labor while those desiring employment are ostracized. Women are by design intuitive and clever, and your courage is already proven. These are fine traits for a whole host of careers, including a physician. Have you told even your mother of your desire to attend medical school?

Miss Harting, of all your endearing qualities I have discovered over this past week, I am honored you shared your intellect without pretense of a passing fancy or overheard comment from a man in your company. Our conversation was a bit of a surprise, but I wanted to assure you it was a most pleasant one. Can I expect more of your impassioned viewpoint tonight?

As I pledge my allegiance to root beer and attempt to sort through the many volumes I must research, my thoughts are on meeting your parents at dinner this evening. Does your father know he raised a woman careful in her appearance yet unruffled by the sand in her shoes after our stroll upon the beach?

Yours sincerely,
Thomas

June 18, 1888.

DEAR BEAUREGARD—

My old friend, how long has it been since we opened a bottle of malt whisky and spent an entire evening searching for the melody in a Russian opera? In many ways not long enough.

Are you again trolling Saratoga for girls eager to annoy overbearing mothers? Or have you contented yourself with the companionship of the Baccarat table? My pleasure involves more than parading through town in a white cycling costume; yet, of anyone I know, you most appreciate a vacation filled with warm sunshine, gay chatter, and a radiant woman. Other than a small obstacle the size of a boulder, your apprentice is faring quite well in California. For the sole purpose of bragging, allow me to share the good parts before humbly asking for your help. And for the record, she agreed to our private outing without any begging.

My new friend, Miss Mary Harting, greeted me in the lobby at sunrise. She had an infectious grin that showed nothing of the early wake-up call. After we shook hands, I motioned for her to sit on a settee and then sat beside her.

She tilted her head. "Why are we sitting down, Thomas? I thought you said the surprise was outside. Aren't you ready to go?"

"Actually, you're not ready yet," I said.

She flattened the pleats around her narrow waist, lifted the hem of her paisley skirt to examine her black boots, and gave a quick tug to each glove. "This is about as ready as I get."

My heart began to pound. I reached across Mary to the end table beside her. She pulled away, but not too far. I felt her warm breath on my neck as I grasped the black scarf I had tucked underneath a crystal ashtray. When I sat back up, Mary plucked the scarf from my hand and held it in her open palm. "Yes, this was definitely too heavy for your pocket. You certainly are smooth."

I should have known better than to try one of your stupid maneuvers.

She wanted to know what I had in mind for the scarf so I explained seeing where we were going would ruin the surprise. I waited for her refusal but instead of a protest, Mary placed the cloth to her eyes and turned. As I slid closer to tie the ends, my hands brushed against her soft hair and I smelled lilac perfume.

Mary took my hand, and I led her out past the gardens and beyond the far side of the hotel. When we stepped into the soft sand, she gripped my forearm.

"Don't worry, I won't let you fall," I said.

"Who said I'm worried *I* might fall? Have you forgotten about the Crown Room where you bumped into me, or the rock you didn't see? Oh, and then there was that branch on the—"

"Okay, you have a point."

She giggled. "I just don't want to go down with the sinking ship."

"Traitor."

I led her across the beach to a narrow path lined with sea grass. As we moved farther from the water's edge, the breeze quieted and I listened to her shallow breath. Neither of us spoke. We were silenced by anticipation.

Though her hand was firm on my arm and I brushed against her shoulders to move branches from her path, when I grasped her waist to keep her from tripping she jumped.

"There was a log," I said.

"My mother warned me about those kinds of logs." She grinned and told me to keep my hands on her elbows.

We continued but I was so nervous that I took her down the wrong path and we had to circle back. Then I realized I missed the trail and had to turn her around again. I was beginning to feel my plan was folly and Mary would demand we return to the hotel when I at last saw the clearing. "We're here," I blurted. I let go of her arm then grabbed it again and made her promise she would wait for my return before removing the handkerchief.

At least a minute passed before I returned to find Mary twirling her thumbs; a sideways smile curled the edge of the blindfold. I wanted to kiss her pastel cheeks.

"Miss Harting, breakfast is served," I said.

In the center of the small clearing was a table draped in white gauze. Yellow rose petals were scattered on and around the table and crystal glasses sparkled in the morning light. Two servers stood beside a cart filled with silver trays and as soon as I nodded, an oboist stepped from the brush and began to play.

"You . . . how . . . this is just lovely, Thomas. When did you have time to plan all this? We've seen each other practically every day for the past two weeks."

"I don't sleep much," I said as I pulled out her chair.

The servers filled our plates with poached eggs, broiled tomatoes, and oranges before Mary cocked her head and stared at me as if she had something to say. When I asked what was on her mind, she adjusted her napkin before answering, "I suppose there is something I'd like to share. I'm just not sure it's going to make any sense."

"Don't let that stop you. You should know by now I'm an expert at not making any sense."

She grinned and said, "Now, that's true." When I

remained silent, Mary rubbed the back of her neck then looked toward the sky. She started by thanking me, but not just for the breakfast. Her gratitude was for our conversations. "It's so nice to speak," she said. "I don't often share my opinion on property taxation or if New York should reinstate the lottery. There's just so much I think about beyond how to wear my hair." She lowered her eyes and looked at me. "Maybe I have too many big ideas, but very few people want to listen, especially to me."

When I complimented her insight and poetic candor she interrupted.

"*And* I've been meaning to talk about all the flattery. You're embarrassing me, even though I sort of enjoyed it . . . the embarrassment I mean. And, well, the compliments too." She shook her head. "See, I told you this was nonsense."

I insisted she continue. Mary chewed on her bottom lip before sharing her wonder over why she let me persist with my compliments. Until that moment I had not thought myself too carried away, but then I am numb from years of listening to your flowery tongue. Mary confessed many sleepless nights before at last arriving at a conclusion.

"Thomas," she said, "you're the only person who's ever really made me a little flustered. I like it. I'm usually stuffed in the corner minding my manners. If I'm asked anything, it's to entertain my parents' friends with piano music and interesting comments on the weather. I've run out of interesting comments on the weather."

"I can imagine," I replied.

"Can you?" She paused and held my gaze. "I think you can. I think it's the writer in you. I've noticed the way you watch people. You get kind of a funny look in your eyes."

Our conversation then turned to books and music and

we chatted with ease and humor. As soon as the plates were cleared, Mary went over to one of the serving girls and whispered in her ear. The server nodded then scampered down the trail toward the hotel. When I asked what she was up to, Mary raised one eyebrow. "Perhaps I have a few tricks of my own," she said.

The girl returned and handed Mary three apples. "If father knew Uncle Donald taught me how to do this, he'd probably never speak to him again."

Mary juggled the apples with the skill of a music-hall performer. As I watched, I felt a warmth rise from the pit of my stomach. Beau, is that how you felt in Rome? Did you have such fascination and admiration you found it almost too much to contain? It was all I could do to keep from sweeping her into my arms.

After the juggling, we left our hideaway and strolled together farther down the path away from the hotel. The trail narrowed and we were forced to crouch under branches and push aside sharp brush. I asked Mary if she wanted to turn back but she was curious to see where the trail ended. Mary took my hand when it was steep, and our trek was rewarded with a vista overlooking the cliffs.

"It's perfect," she said.

I turned to find Mary watching me. "You have some sand," she said. As she brushed my cheek her hand lingered just a second on my chin.

In that moment I wanted to divulge all of my intimate secrets and beg her to do the same. It took great willpower to keep myself from blathering.

After enjoying the view for a few minutes, Mary took a deep breath. "Thomas, I'm so sorry about my father's behavior at dinner. Father hasn't been quite himself this trip. I hope you weren't offended by his smart remarks.

I've asked him to apologize to you personally. I'll be sure and remind him."

I assured her there was no need for her father to apologize in person and was prepared to give an elaborate rationale, when Mary pressed her hand to her forehead. She had forgotten an appointment with her mother and had to get back. As we left, a brisk breeze kicked up sand adding to the melancholy of leaving our intimate view.

We parted at the lobby but met later for dinner. After dessert by the pool, we danced in the ballroom until the orchestra asked us to leave. I debated trying one of your tricks for a goodnight kiss then remembered all the times you were smacked. Still, it was a marvelous day and one I shall never forget. Alas, I fear it is also a night Mary's father will never forget.

After sharing but one awful dinner with Mr. Harting, facing him outside his own suite well beyond a respectable hour made me feel like a nefarious cad. He glared at me before seizing Mary by the elbow and dragging her inside. Before I could apologize for our late night, he slammed the door. This brings us to my boulder.

Meeting Mary's parents was one course shy of a disaster. If the name *Harting* sounds familiar, then you are more astute than your Economics professor gave you credit. The owner of Harting Railways has earned every bit of his grisly reputation.

Beau, as your expertise in such matters is renowned, I must ask. Is there a subtle way to pursue a young lady while dodging her father? I have no desire to spend my vacation anywhere near a man who called me a lazy bummer even before the soup was served.

Your friend in hiding,
Thomas

June 19, 1888.

DEAR MARY—

Recalling the details of yesterday's delightful breakfast brightens this overcast morning. My intent was a quick note to confirm this afternoon's plans, but perhaps this is a good time to squelch any lingering concerns. Seems we have something else in common. Like you, I often find myself making apologies for my father.

When I was a boy, my father was obsessed with the intricacies of language. He required I spend hours in his study with the writings of literary masters like James Fenimore Cooper and Charles Dickens. A typical lad, I was more interested in frog ponds; nevertheless, my father trapped me in his library every afternoon. You can imagine my unending delight during the summer months when the light beckoned through the study window and my friends were turned away at the door.

Upon my eighteenth birthday, Father released me from this responsibility. He is not a sentimental man, and yet on that last day in the study my father's stoic expression turned to one of genuine sadness. In that moment I understood a parent's love is unique and complex, and beyond understanding without firsthand experience. What I am trying to relay in a most round-about way, Mary, is that I understand your father's reaction. His apology, especially in person, is wholly unnecessary.

All fathers are inquisitive of their daughter's acquaintances. Yes, his attitude at dinner was halting, but the restaurant was boisterous and your mother's graceful smile never wavered. If not for my befuddlement at his abrupt contempt for my occupation, I could have better explained my work.

Unlike your father, I will never command a railroad consortium responsible for shaping the economic future of our land, and I have neither the taste for political glory nor the aptitude for science. My ability to turn a phrase, in truth, has little worth in a coal mine, and insinuation I am squandering my family's income is quite familiar. As a matter of record, book sales cover my expenses. True, my novels are far from masterful and plagued with weaknesses artists like Dickens would find an affront to the craft; still, I believe judgment is often cast without proper reflection.

If there were no poets, how would one describe the majesty of a ship's maiden voyage or chronicle the wild landscape of our expansive country? If journalists, editorialists, or even satirists put down their pens, how would we expose marvelous advancements like pasteurization? If society was forbidden fictitious escapes, where would those who must work in coal mines find solace? I conclude, therefore, that without those willing to commit creative words to paper, the very society that values tangibles such as railroad tracks would be without means of acclamation.

Seems my soapbox is out of the closet. I hate to imagine the breadth of this lecture were I not lounging on my balcony eating a raspberry tart.

Now that I have charmed you with a sermon, perhaps we can chat about this over our ice cream this afternoon. There are many who find my profession odd and uncivilized for a proper gentleman. Since you have not commented on my work, should I worry you share this view? Though I have yet to even ask your middle name, I am most interested in your thoughts about my career as a novelist. But as you may find further comment on my regard for your opinion inappropriate, I will save those words for another day.

With respect,
Thomas

June 23, 1888.

DEAR FATHER—

Before you invest in California land, I suggest you plan your own trip west. My schedule does not include sweating in the dingy office of a man who won his campaign by threatening to stuff the ballot box. There are far more interesting activities than "befriending" the new mayor.

For the past three weeks I have embraced the challenge of staying afloat as the sea tries to cast me out. Perhaps you should refrain from sharing this with Mother. She may worry I will be swept out to sea, or worse, seen by an acquaintance in my swimming costume. Dry land, however, is far from tame. Impropriety is found even in this oasis where vulgarity is an unmatched parasol or full hour's wait before procuring a wicker chair on the veranda. Another detail I think well kept from Mother.

You, of course, have heard of the Harting Rails, but I understand you have never met the owner. I suggested you might have crossed paths at a charity event but was corrected in rather gruff and definite terms. He is here on a family vacation, though he is as relaxed as any railroad profiteer. It seems running an empire requires late-night escapades.

Still unable to sleep, I have found warm milk and satisfying gossip with the overnight shift. At one o'clock in the morning I was learning of Wyatt Earp's tawdry gambling hall when Mr. Harting burst into the kitchen. I stood out of his line of sight, but his voice was unmistakable. So was his shrill tone of panic.

Before I could make my presence known, he ordered the staff to unlock the telegram room. One of the domestics offered to summon the operator, but Mr. Harting shoved the man aside and whispered something under his breath.

A maid gasped and ran from the room. Mr. Harting then slammed the door and used the machine himself. A few minutes later he emerged holding a bundle of cash and shoved bills into each of the server's hands. "Lock the door. I was never here."

What sort of legitimate business requires such measures? And who is even awake to receive a telegram at that hour? He is a difficult man, and his actions are even more disconcerting than the inflammatory remarks in your last letter.

Father, it is impossible to be contrary when one is surrounded by strolling violinists and a breeze warmed by the scent of cinnamon. For now I bow to the argument in your letter without rebuttal. If you are rested from your cough (a judgment reserved for Mother), we can debate the effectiveness of violent labor strikes when I return to Boston in August.

Do rest, lest you forget last year I made the mistake of assuming eight-and-twenty was old enough to care for my own crimson nose. Mother was a martinet. While you were in West Virginia speculating on steel mills, I spent days in and out of hot salt baths.

Your son,
Thomas

July 1, 1888.

DEAR AVERY—

In the thick of it now, but the utopian weather is causing delay. How can I write of storms when not a cloud passes? Not to worry; I meet with a rainmaker in the morning.

Thomas

July 1, 1888.

DEAR MARY—

This wonderful month was crowned by a magical evening. Of course, if I told my friend Beauregard about tonight's rendezvous, he would lecture me on the wastefulness of conversation. Beau has a gift for entertaining ladies and likes to think of himself as my mentor. According to his teachings, however, moonlight serves just one purpose.

I apologize if my zealous fawning embarrassed you too much. I expected other guests to stumble upon our garden gazebo, interject a note about the day's fine weather or fresh salmon appetizers and draw my attention from your angelic face. Instead the echo of high tide and the chamber orchestra danced around us in a private, romantic serenade, and I was captivated by the way your pale eyes flared with excitement. If my flattery again too forward, then I have my excuse. But, Mary, you are unlike anyone I have ever met.

Your intellect and convictions give you grace beyond your years. You have thoughtful, knowledgeable opinions yet listen with an open mind and forgiving heart. As you shared your concern for the inhumane conditions in parts of New York, I realized I have never considered the strength of character it takes to leave a homeland and immigrate to a foreign country. Indeed, they deserve our respect and help. How rare it is to find someone so benevolent in a society often cruel and blind to anything but selfish desires. How could I not be captivated by one so passionate and tender?

When I was sixteen I escorted a young lady and her chaperone to my first cotillion. To my dismay, we were also joined by three aunts who found it necessary to straighten the shoulders of my coat and demand I speak up. My mother warned the evening must end at goodnight—this was by far the most needless warning ever given a young lad. At the time I thought my mother feared for our family reputation. I now believe she had a different concern.

A wise man would not hazard writing a note after such a perfect evening, but I was not ready for our time together to end. Instead, I shall thwart orthodoxy and slip this note under your door. My mother would find this impolite and insist I apologize for troubling you. I can only hope I am not troubling you.

Fondly,
Thomas

July 2, 1888.
MARY—
The beach is restless this morning. A stern breeze rattles the café tables stacked by the bar and a thin fog hovers around the shoreline like a boxer waiting for the bell. It is a fitting start to a day without your company. I just wish my note was not the cause of our separation.

As you embark on the city tour with your mother and her homily on decorum, I shall stay locked in my room and try to get some work done. You have derailed me, Miss Harting. I came here to devour a stack of research material and finish the edits on my last novel. Avery has taken to sending daily threats. But how can I work when such a lovely creature is near? Still, I can not blame all of my procrastination on you. Even in your absence there are many distractions. My room affords a generous view.

The stewards have not yet marched out all of the lounges on the veranda so sand glides unfettered across the wooden slats. I see the Roth sisters are poised at the top of the stairs ready to correct any indiscretion on the beach; Mr. Farling is stroking his waxed mustache as he talks with a tall woman in an emerald pelisse; and I have just noticed a young waif by the tearoom. You are indeed correct about my writer's curiosity and propensity for observation.

The girl is pale and wrapped like a rag doll in a cream shawl. Her childish eyes lack an awe of innocence, and fresh tears dampen her sunken cheeks as she stares at a gent throwing rocks into the sea. Is she weeping over a troubled past? Perhaps she had trusted a man's sweet lies and now mourns the sin of passion.

On that fretful day, she found herself soaked and shivering in the moss-covered doorway of the home she wished to avoid. She had always thought fate mischievous, but she clung to her juvenile ideals of love. His declarations were more powerful than the sense God had granted, and she now lamented her carnal sin.

A light appeared in the window and she wanted to flee before he found her with her hair in long wet tangles and her clothes pressed to her frail shape. Yet her mind was as murky as the bogs. The door opened, and he stood at the threshold. Even in the dim light she saw the loathsome thoughts his eyes failed to conceal.

She took a step back, but he seized her forearm and she had no choice but to go inside and meet the woman for whom he had promised his love before God. She wished she could instead thrust a sword into her heart.

Mary, do you think this is an interesting opening for a novel? My literary life began by observing others, creating imaginary lives from noticing a raised brow or wrinkled collar. I have never shared the start of my writing career with anyone—not even with my good friend, professor, and mentor Henry James. I would like you to meet him someday, provided you do not gush over his well-deserved popularity. His ego is sufficient for a man his height.

When I started at Harvard, I felt at last freed from my father's tether and therefore pursued anything contradictory to his rhetoric. Though not proud of my youthful exuberance, I admit membership in the Viking Council of the Mystic Brotherhood. We were a boisterous lot of privileged wastrels serving mankind by proclaiming edicts and charming pretty ladies. Moreover, I blame the brotherhood for my appalling turnabout from the pursuit of a respectable law degree.

During one of our weekly meetings at Horatio's Beanery, a rum-hole popular with all sorts of contrary college clubs, I noticed two men arguing. Shouting matches were commonplace at the Beanery, but these men were too engrossed and well beyond the age of college.

The elder was red-faced, leaning forward with the linen tablecloth clasped in his fist. The younger man was slumped in his chair as his gaze wavered about the room in obvious disobedience. At once I recognized the tension between a father and son (my area of expertise), so I bid my friends good night, ordered a glass of scotch, and gawked. A habit developed in preparatory school, I carry a small pad and pencil in my breast pocket. Before I was even aware of it, the pad was on the bar and I was taking notes.

The son's hair was mussed as if he had started to run his hands through it but changed his mind lest his father see weakness in his frustration. His clothes were pressed, but there were bread crumbs on his vest that neither noticed, and several times the father folded his arms across his chest and checked his watch.

I noticed other details too; the way the forks scraped against the dinner plates in the rhythm of the father's hands; the waiter's padded steps against the worn paths in the carpet; and the sharp musk of cheap cologne and spilled whiskey. My hand trembled as I wrote it all down like a witness unable to turn away from a gruesome accident.

That night I went back to my dormitory and wrote a short story about the scene. It was my first attempt at anything more creative than a legal brief, so when the draft was finished I tucked it under my bed. For the first time in my life I was unable to sleep. Law classes continued, but suddenly I could not focus on due process. I edited and reworked my tale until I thought it a masterpiece. When a stunned classmate agreed to read it, I was devastated by his review.

I envisioned him falling to his knees and proclaiming my genius before rushing to share my story with our friends. Instead, he laughed and warned me to stay away from scotch. My efforts thwarted, I put down my pen until one morning I bolted upright from a crushing pain in my chest. At once I knew it was the unperfected pages tucked in the drawer. I also knew what I had to do. That afternoon I changed my major to English Literature and altered the course of my life. It took the next several years, however, to realize the consequences of that decision.

Strange that I should keep something so unremarkable secret, though I suppose we all choose to veil what makes us most uncomfortable. What I find remarkable is that I am at ease sharing such an intimate experience with you. This is perplexing for a man who works for months in solitude, so perhaps I should change the subject, lest this new found candor is beyond my control—an unsettling thought for any man.

Will you sail with me tomorrow? I have let a fine, thirty-four-foot sloop with a spinnaker and two-man crew. All men from New England know how to captain a ship. I guarantee my skills are capable enough that we shall not run aground or drown at sea. And before you ask, yes, I have a motive. Sailing is a vigorous sport and every man must prove himself successful in something other than a conversation.

Thomas

July 11, 1888.

DEAR HENRY—

Persuasion to sit at your poker table is quite unnecessary. My fortune is your rotten luck. Having worthy news without knowing whom to tell is an odd dilemma. Consequence waits for a fragile moment, so I fear being too hasty in my revelation. As a regimented writer I know you understand my resolve, although perhaps you should examine if such rigid habits ruin your card game.

I will get to my point without unnecessary delay even though I so enjoy knowing vague, long-winded tales turn you red. Her name is Mary, and I am the worst kind of fool. I am the man we have criticized for weakness of character and an indiscriminant nature. Yet I have never been so excited.

Mary is enchanting. Every infatuated male believes his ladylove is captivating, so I hope to let your own eyes be the judge and will forgo the clichés of flower petals and reflective pools. I know you are disappointed. As the characters in your well-written prose, she is best described by her actions and abilities, so I shall do my best to be sincere even though my perspective is most biased.

She plays the pianoforte with a light musical touch and pursues politics with the intuition of a statesman. She has a sharp wit; is courageous devoid of bravado; sips champagne without getting hiccups; and I have witnessed a quiet disagreement with a most cantankerous man who lost his point then thanked her for a charming evening.

Although she has a delicate pen, she proclaims elaborate letters a frustration. I believe this to be her hand's inability to keep up with her quick mind. Mary also loves to read and is one of your many fans, Mr. James. Moreover, she claims to enjoy the bits of scrawl I have shown her and believes writing is a noble profession.

At yesterday's afternoon tea, Mary's elbow relation joined our intimate party. She had the eyes of an owl, and her sporadic reach for the sugar agitated my nerves. Never fond of an overly inquisitive nature, I was in a pucker after enduring a litany of personal questions. I feared she might soon ask my preference in undergarments. After several polite attempts to thwart the inquisition, Mary did something I have never witnessed in polite conversation. At that moment my interest and admiration were transformed into something worthy of this letter.

In one delicate motion Mary placed her hand over her cousin's mouth and said, "Your interest in Mr. Gadwell borders that of a drooling meddler. I wouldn't want your reputation ruined by your overzealous enthusiasm."

She then turned to me and said, "I'm confident you aren't offended by strong family bonds, Mr. Gadwell, and simply need to clear your throat to regain a proper tone. Then maybe you'll share the charming story about your adventures in Edinburgh with only a toothbrush and outdated map."

Tea was rather enjoyable after that.

Is it transparent I am putting Mary's favors to paper more for myself than your amusement? After knowing her little more than a month I would be a ninny not to question such irrational and powerful feelings for a woman who was seasick not ten miles from the shore. Still, I feel quite rational. My purest desire is that you are someday as much a halfwit. Of course, as you like to point out, bliss comes with a price.

You sent me here to focus on my writing and yet I am more distracted than ever. Your long-winded sermons on discipline vibrate in my head, and I would promise to try harder if you were not so well acquainted with my habits.

For now I leave you to worry for my career and chastise me among our friends. I know you are a decent fellow and feel confident my words fall upon fair, if not gentle ears. As you have endured my mother's excitable nature and my father's scorn, my request is that you refrain from sharing any of this with my parents before you leave on your encore book tour for *The Portrait of a Lady.* Once I have claimed Mary's affection, which we both know to be inevitable given my formidable charm and modest manner, I shall brave calamity by introducing Mary to my parents.

Yours, in friendship,
Thomas

July 15, 1888.

MY DEAR MARY—

Unspoken desires smolder in the stillness before the sunrise. But the subtle glow is not a glimpse of the day to rise; it is what lingers from the evening past.

Last night I commented on your exquisite ball gown when I longed to say you are exquisite. Had we found a quiet moment away from the seaside gala, I would have taken your hand in mine and described the loveliest woman I have ever met.

If it were just your outer beauty, I would have the capacity to admire and go my way. But your splendor goes beyond a fair complexion, graceful manner, and smile that glows from warmth of spirit. Your mind is sharp without insult and your elegance most noted not by dress or practiced refinements, but the quiet intellect that displays your guile while complementing everyone around you.

Until now I have kept my writing, my work, in the shadows out of fear and greed. Yet your enthusiasm for the creative will is like a new beam in a sunken roof. Now that you are in my thoughts, I wonder if I shall ever write anything but a romance novel. Never have I so longed to share intimate details and secret passions; never have I so desired to share myself with another.

During one of our many turns around the ballroom floor, you asked me what I see in the future. I must confess, I was relieved by your father's abrupt intrusion, for your question deserves more than the witless comment I would have spouted in my panic. Before we met six weeks ago, the answer to your question was simple.

After the summer, I am to return to Boston to meet with my agent, check on estate affairs, and argue with my father. As I have bored you with numerous retellings, you already know about the expected contract for my second novel. This means I must rush off to our family home in Newport to preoccupy myself with drafting a third book before I decide to re-read my second novel and am overcome with the desire to re-write what has in error been declared finished. For months I shall shut myself off from the world to agonize over each syllable until I drive myself mad and escape for a rest.

I have just stopped to review this prattle; you must now think me a dullard. You know these trivialities, and yet I find it easier to blather than search for a true answer. It seems until now I have not thought much beyond wild literary success. Meeting you has forced me to reconsider, and your inquiry deserves a more appropriate answer.

As I take a few moments to reflect on these wonderful days by the sea, I now foresee knowing all of the porters' names on the train from Boston to New York and learning to navigate the streets to your door with ease. There are grand family parties with a most remarkable woman on my arm and wonderful moments we will someday murmur behind cupped hands. Perhaps the details are thin, but my feelings for you are true. Mary, you asked what I see ahead, and the answer is you.

I must stand unashamed for an honest answer to your question. Do I dare now ask the same question of you?

With deep affection,

Thomas

July 16, 1888.
DEAR AVERY—
No rain, though I looked dashing in a feathered headdress. Fear not, I am undaunted. Below the bluffs is a treacherous seaside cavern where the crashing waves sound like thunder.

I return to Boston in a few weeks and hope to have news to share. I will contact you the moment I arrive. For now I just need rope, a harness, and a guide willing to dangle me off a cliff. Were you here, I suspect you would volunteer for the job.

Your fearless,
Thomas

July 16, 1888.

MY DEAREST MARY—

Be warned, fair maiden, you have opened your heart to a writer and what we mean to say often has no voice. We are left with time and ink.

It was the softness of her lips that stirred his thoughts. Perfection was as sand in the breeze, for the soul is most vulnerable when faced with loss. The devil may be no more than the messenger of sorrowful news for those too afraid of what love requires. Step lively, the wise boy tells himself, for a gift this precious may not be offered a second time.

It was her trembling hands that said more than her declarations of passion. They danced, as they had many other nights, but why did she feel fragile in his arms? Why were their words so stilted, labored and confounded on a night of such rejoicing? He knew that for their wisp of time among the trees, happiness was now so dependent on another. They must trust when instinct tells them to hide away.

It was her smile as they parted that changed him forever. Love is not as the sonnet, fancy with blooming roses and dancing violins. The imagination of love is such things. Love is contentment in moments of silence; the peaceful warmth from her touch, so foreign the first time; and the unrestrained grin recalling a shared moment of folly.

How blessed this undeserving boy, how truly blessed.

Yours,
Thomas

July 20, 1888.

DEAREST—

When your father refused me at your door this morning, I feared your mother was ill. Never did I expect such rash action. My dear, you need not apologize for his insolence. You were so pale from the shock—can you forgive *me* for not overcoming my own disbelief to comfort you?

I must know why your father demands you end your vacation and return to New York tomorrow. By now your father must have read my note. I am off to search the grounds so I can better explain my honorable intentions to him in person. I will not stand idle as the woman I adore is snatched from my arms. Your father was once a young man in love. Surely, that man will listen to reason.

Your love,
Thomas

July 31, 1888.

DEAR BEAU,

Thank you. I needed the swift kick.—Thomas

August 1, 1888.

MY DARLING—

Even after ten days for reflection, I am still quite stunned that your father refused to speak to me even as I stood right in front of him. It would have been less insulting had he shoved me to the ground and stepped on my coat. Though I know your mother wishes I were a duke with castles across the pond, at least she accepted my hand and bid me farewell. As your train pulled away you were so dignified that for a moment I felt nothing but pride. I wish that emotion had lasted; what came next was less than gallant.

With you on your way home, I spent long nights in the Babcock Lounge with Simon and his tall glasses of cognac. This ended with my head slumped against the pinewood bar, followed by Simon helping me to my room as I demanded to know how life could continue without your angelic glow to light the unknown path ahead. I must leave him a handsome tip. Unlike the overindulgence in brandy, where all of humanity is dismal, cognac is best when one desires a more personal disdain. Of course no indulgence is left unpunished; my head throbbed as hard as my heart after our first dance. I shut myself in my room and refused even Walter's assistance. After two days with the curtains drawn, I received good advice from a friend and my inherent optimism was unleashed.

Miss Mary Winnifred Harting, you agreed to continue our affair. As adults in a free society I see no reason to alter our resolve. New York is a city of strangers where a man of average height is anonymous and a woman's face is easily hidden by the latest fashion. We shall take full advantage of your vast city as we give your father time to calm down. As for my parents, I have given this considerable thought.

I think it best to postpone introductions. My father is quite fond of moral platitudes and my mother, a loving and genteel woman, once decided to throw Father a surprise birthday party then asked him what kind of cake he wanted. Discretion is our most advantageous path.

So, dearest, I have packed our memories alongside the penny postcards and shell-encrusted fruit bowl for my parents and leave tomorrow. I promise my next letters shall be filled with an ingenious scheme for our secret rendezvous. I must also warn that the cognac seems to have had a lasting effect. I plan on spending the train ride to New York dreaming of your tender lips and masterminding how I shall steal a kiss.

Your adoring,
Thomas

FALL 1888

August 5, 1888.

DEAR MARY—

Is it true God speaks to a man with his own rail car? According to the *New York World,* a private rail car has marble sinks, gold chandeliers, stout fireplaces, and a ne'er-do-well flopped against the bar claiming he never sported an Imperial beard in his youth. The C. P. Huntington is not quite as well appointed; though I believe we too can boast of freeloaders aboard.

I take comfort in my own compartment with a private shower, a full oil lamp, and a quaint bed that would fit quite well if I were three inches shorter. The dining car offers tasty silver cake but has run out of Earl Grey. The linens are a fine blend; the observation car has lush leather club chairs; and the porter gave me a bottle of unbranded hair oil compliments of Union Pacific. Can you smell me from New York? Ladies have taken to walking the passageway with handkerchiefs over their noses. However, my unfortunate choice in men's furnishings does not explain why your letterbox is empty.

Four days have passed since I last penned your name, yet the delay was not from lacking something to say. By now you know I am seldom without words. I could tell you I desired time for thoughtful reflection, but I admit I needed the train stop in the Utah territory.

I, of course, understand if you no longer wish to consort with a man who, unable to locate a mere scrap, incurred a hefty fine for writing a letter on the tablecloth. I blame my senselessness on what I must stare at all day.

How impassive it is to dismiss the barren flats from the vantage of passing by. But even after a second viewing, I find the remote, scorched plains redundant to the point of exhaustion. The rush to settle all thirty-eight states is best left to men more desirous of land ownership than a hot bath. Alas, indifference has left time for wandering thoughts.

It is senseless to ruminate about your father's rash actions and hostile mood while stuck on this jarring steel box without any way to receive your letters. Still, I keep thinking about his preoccupation with business and the forceful hold on your arm as he pulled you through the lobby. As I admit my apprehension (blackmail you will someday use to enlist my help in choosing lace curtains), it seems the neighbors are again drawing blood.

A young mother and her two boys are in the adjacent sleeper. Through the walls I hear the boys wrestle over marbles while their mother insists they work on their McGuffey Readers. In truth, I enjoy listening to their familiar antics. They give me pause to remember the feeling of rolling down grassy knolls and imagining you as a child.

I envision your leather toecap shoes dangling from the kitchen stool as you gobbled chocolate ice cream and taught your cook to read. You had the face of a cherub with a sharp mind scorned by headmistresses concerned for your proper station. Someday you must further explain how you developed such strong opinions while in the oppressiveness of Port Chester Preparatory School for Girls.

Young ladies are depicted dressing dolls and sipping tea with pristine gloved hands. This is absurd. A woman able to throw a rock straight across the sea must have seen many days with dirty gloves.

As for the young lad my good friends called Gads, I was a quiet boy with a talent for mischief behind a credulous, thoughtful gaze. Of course this appearance did not fool a mother ready with punishment even before the offense occurred. The last anyone called me Gads, I avoided my own reader. To now think of the nickname brightens a tiresome ride indeed. Will you indulge me? I can not explain the actions of senseless boys but do suggest you may learn why you rightfully crossed the street to avoid passing too close.

Like most boys of ten, I was fearless and slapdash, and in the endless summer of 1869 I spent all my time with three great friends.

Our leader, Malcolm Weston, stood a solid four inches taller than the rest of us and had a straightforward likeable manner. As neighbors, we played since infancy but my father compared our differences to the Republicans and Greenbacks.

Unlike Malcolm, with his thin frame, unruly blond hair, and deep-set green eyes that girls found *alluring* when we entered puberty, my smooth dark hair and round features did not suit me until well past puberty. Still, most found me as agreeable as Malcolm. And as the planner, my creative ideas always found an enthusiastic home with my good friend.

Talkative twin brothers, Gregory and William Crawley, moved from Baltimore earlier that year. They finished each other's sentences and did fantastic tricks like walking on their hands and flips in the air. Malcolm and I could only tell them apart by the way William's right nostril flared as he spoke. Even then I knew girls considered Gregory and William handsome by the way the girls pushed past me to talk to them. But the brothers preferred frog ponds and flips to the fairer sex, and that suited Malcolm and me quite well.

Early that summer the four of us felt the need for a men's club, a hamlet where we could discuss such weighty matters as the best kite design. Buckley Pond was no more than a swimming hole and less than a mile from our city homes, but as we spent long afternoons lounging under the sweet gum trees, it seemed fitting to design a tree house with a lakefront view. We drew detailed plans in the mud, and our ambitious sketch included a generous porch, peaked roof, and a swinging saloon door. The James-Younger Gang enthralled us. It turned out our gang was just as ill-fated.

We began our tree house with discarded oak planks and various kindling snuck from Malcolm's carriage house. After using enough nails to build the White House, and then sealing the wood with a sticky paste William concocted from tree sap and pond water, the frail limbs of the gum trees would not hold the weight of the wood. This is most obvious now.

After a debate in the form of wrestling, we agreed upon a shoreline cabana and the plans were revised. Because we wanted a sturdy clubhouse, we set our support beams in the pliable mud. Persistence surmounted our architectural prowess.

Construction continued through rain; mosquitoes; the death of one unfortunate frog due to William's bad aim with a hammer; bleeding fingers; Malcolm's brainless use of poison ivy as a wood filler; too many splinters to count; and even imprisonment in my father's study. Two weeks after the second plans were drawn, we had a lopsided box without windows, a door that would not swing, the imagination of a porch because William cut the opening on the wrong side, and space enough for four if one of us sat halfway out the door. That slowest sod, usually Gregory, had to make up new excuses why his knee breeches were so muddy.

Though on occasion a board would splash into the water, I loved our fort; we all did. It was a haven where we dreamt up adventures and laughed at silly jokes. Our young wits could not understand what we had truly built and why it was, and still is, so special. Within those shaky walls we captured our youthful perspectives on life; priceless ideals we are forced or feel ready to toss away then want back when youth is gone. Ours are preserved to recall on days such as these. I would say it was a productive summer indeed.

Like all summer holidays it ended with deep sadness, and the cold weather came on quick and harsh. That was the winter smallpox was discovered in our area. Just after Thanksgiving, Gregory Crawley fell sick. He died the day before Christmas.

Malcolm, William, and I went back to our fortress after Gregory's funeral for our own sort of memorial, but discovered it too had fallen with the onset of winter. Just a few weeks later Malcolm was shipped off to spend a semester at a German boarding school and William's father moved the family to Worcester. When Malcolm returned, we continued our friendship, but we never spoke of that summer or of our fort. It was as if the memory, too precious or too painful, was best kept locked in our minds.

I have not thought of Gregory's death in years. To picture him in his Sunday suit, his arms folded across his chest and his lips puckered, I feel just as overwhelmed by death as I did then. The preacher praised God for Gregory's new beginning, but my friend lay motionless in a black box while his mother sobbed and his brother sat fixed and vacant.

Perhaps the motion of the train stirs more than the chicken fricassee, as my intent was not so melancholy. Though thinking about one's passing is a reminder to seize every moment. In five days, I intend to do just that.

With love,
Thomas

August 12, 1888.

DEAR AVERY—

My good man, you will never believe what happened. Then again, you once dined with William Hearst so maybe you will. I am in New York on assignment. That I gave myself the assignment is inconsequential and well explains my continued tardiness.

On the train from California I sat right beside Black Bart, the infamous stagecoach robber. Of course he never revealed his identity, but he quoted poetry, wore a long linen duster, and carried a blanket roll. Who else could it have been? The mysterious man feigned surprise at my desire to do an interview, but you are the one who stresses tenaciousness. So I am in pursuit. I lost him in Grand Central Station but the trail is warm. Soon you shall not only have the final edits for the second book but a once in a lifetime perspective sure to make front-page headlines. Just think of the publicity.

Thomas

August 14, 1888.

DEAR MOTHER—

Did you know your dear cousin Penelope is enamored with Eastman's new camera? She snapped photos of me posed on her fainting couch until my vision, and dignity, were quite blurred. All the same, her antics are loveable and I appreciate her graciousness at accepting an unannounced guest. New York City is even livelier than you remember.

Harried shoppers swarm bright, glass-front stores, and the sidewalks are covered with plaster dust from new marble-faced buildings. Policemen in wide straw hats direct a confusion of buggies and pedestrians, and during peak hours the streetcar bells and whistles are deafening. The excitement has no equal, yet the frenzy reminds me of you and Aunt Ruth after a second pot of tea. Fashionable elite do still stroll through the parks swinging jade parasols; however, arduous dinner parties with insufferable guests are most stylish. Last night I returned from such a dismal evening and interrupted Penelope with a suitor.

By the red faces and stammering, I surmise your cousin is quite smitten. Mr. Lancaster is a reputable banker and, like Penelope, lost his spouse before there were any children. He is forthright, polite, and very much in love with your cousin. You need not ask. I will do my best to find out more and, ever the dutiful son, write in generous detail. Until then, I am indebted to an understanding mother who is content to know I am well without badgering to know why I changed my plans.

Your loving son,
Thomas

August 18, 1888.
DEAR HENRY—
Your book tour sounds as flawless as your enthusiasm for London, though your thrashing of Americans' plebeian use of sugar nippers is objectionable. I hope you do not forgo Boston for the glamour of dining with royalty. As I am in New York, Mother forwarded your letter. You are a man of great intelligence and can fit the puzzle together for yourself. Unlike your tour, however, my excursion is so far anything but congenial. In fact, in just twenty-four hours I was thrown to the curb twice.

On the train from California to New York, Mother's indoctrination on the virtues of honor and thank-you notes rattled through my head, supplanting my impulse for scheming. So with coal still in my hair, I went straight to Mary's door to inquire on her family's health and wellbeing. Mary was seated in the parlor. Upon my entrance she jumped to her feet, startled to see me, then gave a polite bow. She looked exquisite in a lavender velvet jacket yet remained distracted and fidgeted with the lace trimming on her sleeves. As usual, my timing was deplorable.

Mrs. Harting was also in the parlor. She was upset about a broken platter and made her disgust of my sudden, unannounced company well-known. After inquiring several times as to the reason and length of my stay, Mrs. Harting rang for a servant to dispatch a messenger to Mr. Harting and escort me to the door. You can understand my surprise and elation to receive an invitation for dinner at the Harting home that evening. I still lament my optimism lasted but a few hours.

My waistcoat pressed and boots shined, I was ready to at last have a fruitful conversation and greeted Mary's father with a strong handshake and straight back. In return, Mr. Harting introduced me to Mary's escort for the evening, Mr. Lowell Kennard.

Lowell Kennard is a slight man with black hair and a deep red scar on his cheek that emphasizes his pale skin. His face looks menacing with fresh creases and converging grey circles around dark eyes. I guessed his age nearing forty. Though a Harting Railway employee, Mr. Kennard acted like the biggest toad in the puddle, with a ruffled dinner shirt and pert white carnation tucked in his lapel. His growing wealth and status were impressive; however, *my sort* (as was referenced with vigor) has little patience for a man with arms long enough to pat himself on the back. After introductions, Kennard ignored the other guests and insisted Mary give him a private tour of the solarium. I had a new objective for the evening.

Seated across from Mary and Kennard during dinner, I watched him brush her hand while reaching for the salt and feign the need to lean close to hear her speak. Fragments of the dinner conversation swarmed around me as I sat like a bronze bust. It took all of my willpower to keep from leaping across the pot roast and seizing Kennard's scrawny neck. My silence might have gone unnoticed if not for Mr. Harting's request that I pass the gravy. When I responded with a vacant stare, Mr. Harting reached around the guest beside me, slapped me across the face, and said, "Good God, Gadwell, are you suffering hysterical paralysis from the train?" More fun was still to come.

Dinner ended without my spilling anything on the carpet; then I followed the others into the living room. Mr. Kennard positioned himself beside Mary while the rest of the intimate party found chairs around the room. Seizing an opportunity when Mr. Harting was forced into the empty seat beside me, I at last spoke. I wished I had kept my mouth shut.

"Mr. Harting, sir, dinner was delicious, sir, and it's so nice to see you relaxed now that you're home. You seemed a little vexed at the hotel." Without even a glance in my direction, he got up and stood by the window.

There was one moment when I caught Mary's eye, but Mr. Kennard forced her attention when he tapped her arm. "Are you enjoying the unseasonable weather, Mary? Do you think the warm temperatures will ruin our colorful fall foliage?"

"I haven't really given it any thought, Mr. Kennard, but that's an interesting question. What do you think?"

Mr. Kennard leaned toward her. "I certainly hope not. It's the leaves that make this time of year so enchanting. You mentioned your fondness for gardens. I would think this is your favorite time of year. It is mine. Do we have that in common, Mary? And, please, I won't ask again, you must call me Lowell."

The deliberateness in his presentation left me unsettled. I got to my feet and approached Kennard with a wide grin.

After the smallest of talk, Mr. Kennard asked about my occupation then waited until the coffee was served to find out what I had published and patronize why he had never heard of my work. As a rule, this conversation takes place between the artichoke salad and glazed ham.

To keep his attention, I asked what he did for Mr. Harting. He took a sip of his coffee while keeping his eyes on Mary then said, "I'm not here to discuss business."

"So why are you here, Mr. Kennard? I find it curious an employee was invited to such a private gathering." It was not my best attempt at subtlety, but I was under extreme duress.

He looked at me, or rather up at me, given the great difference in our height. "I assure you I was invited, Mr. . . ."

"Gadwell."

He shrugged. "I'm here because Mr. Harting is a true patriot. You obviously didn't fight in the war, but I enlisted at the tender age of fourteen and braved scenes someone of your sort can't even imagine. This scar," he brushed his cheek, "was from an enemy bullet. I never wept, not once. I was incredibly brave."

I mumbled a polite reply, but he was again staring at Mary, so I asked him to share his war stories. My plan to keep him talking to me lasted just a few minutes. This was when Mr. Harting strode to the center of the room.

"Guests, you must hear my darling daughter play. Mary, come. And, Mr. Kennard, why don't you turn pages."

Kennard bowed and rushed to the piano.

For twenty minutes Mary slid away from Kennard's increasing interest in the sheet music while Mary's father, the conspirator, was not even in the room. After the recital, Mary escaped with the ladies to the sewing room while I remained with the men in the study. Cigars were passed around, and I watched Mr. Harting hold a match for Mr. Kennard. This seemed out of character for the man I met in California. Then the most unusual incident went unnoticed by everyone but me.

When Mr. Harting again excused himself, I retreated to the corner to brood and keep an eye on Mr. Kennard. Kennard stood alone by the window checking the weather while the other men smoked cigars in small groups. Unaware of my position, Kennard glanced around to see if anyone was watching, then he slipped an empty glass ashtray into his jacket pocket. A smirk skated across his face before he returned to the group predicting a pleasant ride home.

Why in the world would Kennard steal a worthless ashtray? Why would he steal anything? My dislike for the man is understandable, but rivalry aside, there is something odd about Lowell Kennard.

The ladies returned before I could question Kennard. Then, just when I spotted Mary, the butler grabbed my arm and escorted me to the front door. I was tossed out at just nine o'clock, leaving Mary and Kennard to conclude the evening alone. That was one of the longest nights of my life.

Henry, a messenger just delivered a note. Mr. Harting demands I join him for lunch tomorrow. After his disinterest at dinner, what could he want? The idea his attitude has changed so quickly is beyond even my optimism. I find myself wondering if he also summoned Mr. Kennard, like a bloody clash orchestrated by the King. And I forgot to pack my armor.

With respect,
Thomas

August 26, 1888.

HENRY—

Our letters crossed and I just received your note asking for my assistance. I am humbled. It is a fine compliment for the teacher to need the student, even if the subject of your telegram was startling. The illicit plot you recounted reads like one of your works of fiction. To be honest, I imagined your voice husky from countless engagements in front of large lecture halls, not from shouting in over-filled parlors. With all the colorful bloomers and high-pitched giggling, are you certain of what you overheard?

From your description, it sounds like your colleague was deceived by a clever crooked cross. As you suggested, a scheme to forge and sell U.S. bonds requires remarkable ingenuity; however, your puzzlement in how such a con could succeed comes from an erroneous assumption. Bonds are not traceable. Like currency, ownership of a bond is based on possession and is not in any way recorded or monitored. To now think about it, counterfeit bonds are in fact an ideal swindle.

Treasury bonds are purchased at a discount to their face value and mature with time. They are meant to be held, sometimes as long as thirty years, and are preferred by wealthy investors looking to diversify. A mark would not even know he was fooled until it was too late, and who better to defraud into purchasing a fake bond than a foreigner who has never seen a real one?

Seems I have learned a bit from my father over the years. Though I have no suggestion for your friend other than the legal measures you mentioned, I hope this is the clarification you needed. Be careful, Henry. Idle pleasures are indeed tempting, and you will find greedy men are miserly in all aspects of life. I shall never forget the summer when I was one-and-twenty and lured by such fancies. Beware the time spent with those driven by their own importance. I should think this an obvious caution for one so level-headed, but you are toasting success with those corrupted by pride. Hold fast to your moral compass; the gravity pulls hard around such men.

As we are speaking of ruthless sorts, I met Mary's father for lunch. It turned out the compelling atmosphere of Delmonico's matched our conversation. That, however, was all that was well matched.

I arrived at noon as instructed. Mr. Harting was not yet seated in the men's café, so I wandered to the bar and ordered iced tea. The first floor was crowded with prominent businessmen and fashionable parvenus admiring the view through enormous windows overlooking the flower beds in front of Madison Square Garden. Comments on the new chandeliers, obviously of German craftsmanship, were bested by postulating whether American imposters frescoed the ceiling and if the beef filet was tender. Other than an elderly woman near the stairway that led to the bachelor apartments above, the room reeked of men.

After waiting ten minutes I must have looked tense because a gent in a white Panama hat flopped on the next stool, ordered me a rum (which I declined but later regretted), and told me there were swans in the banquet hall. Before he could elaborate, Mr. Harting arrived and we were shown to a table set for two. I checked my pocket watch as I unfolded my napkin, but Mr. Harting made no apology for his tardiness. Instead, he waved to a waiter and ordered both of our meals without consulting the menu or me.

Charlton Harting is a bulky man, with thick palms and a long forehead. It is quite fortunate that Mary looks like her mother. Sitting face to face with a railroad lord made me feel like a jester before the king, and, still, there was a sense of power at our table. Others were sneaking glances, wondering if I was, in fact, lunching with a volatile madman. As Mr. Harting launched into a monologue, he seemed quite sane.

I considered sharing his speech with you but could not bring myself to write in such graphic and offensive slang. The gist of Mr. Harting's story is that his father was a railway gandy dancer who weaned young Charlton upon the steam beasts. With skill, and the plain admission of good fortune, Mr. Harting consolidated a few struggling lines and turned his hard work into a successful enterprise. He spoke with a lilting fondness for the early years that were vibrant for a young entrepreneur. The rails made him wealthy, but he confessed bitterness for an industry now plagued with enormous debt and ongoing labor strikes. While his idioms would cause my mother to swoon, he seemed sincere and forthright. So much so, I was encouraged. As soon as the salad arrived, however, his demeanor changed and *madman* again crossed my mind.

Mr. Harting pushed his plate aside, narrowed his eyes, and leaned forward placing both elbows on the table. "I forbid you to ever see my daughter again."

I grinned. You know the one, Henry, my uncontrollable grimace when I get nervous. My top lip even stuck to my front teeth.

"I can see you're as foolish as I thought, so let me make this simple. I'm her father, and I want you to leave Mary alone. Is that clear enough for a Harvard boy? Mary was sweet-talked by a smooth dickens looking for a little fun on vacation, but a wastrel in a silk cravat is easily forgotten. She's young and doesn't know what she needs. I know what she needs, and rest assured, Gadwell, it's not you."

"Sir—"

"Real men, men with grease under our nails, have a saying. 'If you can't make the grade then dump some of your load before you ruin the engine.' Some pansy with a sharp tongue isn't going to ruin my engine. You got that? Not when—"

"Sir, I'd like to—"

He slammed his fist on the table. "I'm not here for a discussion. I don't give a fig about you or what you have to say. This is your one and only warning to stay away from Mary. I have eyes everywhere, Gadwell, and they're watching you. If you need proof, I'll gladly let you talk to a friend of mind. I think you've heard of Johann Most, though I'd hate to bother him with such an insignificant matter."

He looked at me hard, just as I imagined Johann Most looked at that young father before pushing him from a bridge during the Haymarket Riot. Without blinking, Mr. Harting signaled for the waiter.

"We're done here," Mr. Harting said. Though he had spoken to the server, his words were meant for me. As the young man cleared our untouched salad plates, Mr. Harting commented on the pleasant weather before canceling the Veal Piccata and asking for the bill.

He checked the time on his own pocket watch and adjusted the brown Coachman he had forgotten to remove in his rush to erase me from the family scrapbook. Then he again looked at me as if he would shove me into the street if I got in his way.

"Gadwell, I'm not a patient man. For Mary's sake, and only her sake, you have until tonight to leave the city." Then he shrugged and added, "If I haven't made everything plain for a dandy boy like you, then I guess you'll just have to learn the hard way . . . very hard."

At this point the hero would leap to his feet, proclaim his love, and refuse to leave. I have never proclaimed myself a hero but wanted to believe I would act as one if the circumstance arose. My disappointment still stings.

I mumbled something about leaving but omitted any mention of not seeing Mary again. This seemed sufficient, as Mr. Harting left without another word or paying the bill.

Henry, Mary's father carries on as if I am a penniless libertine with a scandalous reputation and wooden leg while he befriends a violent anarchist suspected of murder. This of course brings up how in the world Mr. Harting knows such a man. The whole episode was so implausible. Plus, his blasted overreaction has turned us into frauds.

I told Mary her father was still irritable and suggested I leave New York. Neither of us wanted to say goodbye, so Mary and I have been sneaking around the city. Rendezvousing at dusk and slipping into the theatre after the curtain rises is not the courtship I envisioned, though it has some thrills. Still, my quest for Mary's hand now rests on patience, faith, and watching around corners for Mr. Harting's many keen eyes.

With admiration,
Thomas

P.S.—You do also believe Mr. Harting's threat was just the bravado of an overprotective father?

August 27, 1888.

DEAR AVERY—

I lost Black Bart at a flea market. Who knew coach robbers liked porcelain cats. However, all is not lost. As I write this I am having breakfast in the same café as President Hayes. His term may be long over, as evidenced by his grey beard and cane, but think of the useful fodder I could learn from an ex-Commander-in-Chief.

I must go. Hayes is on the move. Believe it or not, I think he just slipped out without leaving a tip.

Thomas

September 7, 1888.

BEAU—

Your invitation to spend the winter in the Greek Islands is gracious but unnecessary. Stunning creatures are not just found abroad.

Refrain from telling the story about losing the hotel keys on the Lisbon beach, and if you need my assistance in writing a love poem to sweeten a foreign disposition, I am at your disposal. In return, perhaps you could share your knowledge about evasion techniques and disguises. And before you ask, no, the man lurking at my corner is not an irate lover. I believe you have that market cornered.

Safe travels,

Thomas

September 10, 1888.

DEAR HENRY—

While you have spent a month exploring the lush English countryside and promoting your work, Mary and I have enjoyed every possible moment together. Though cautious, we play the role of lovers as we stroll through the city's tireless park and dine in secluded restaurants. Yet I am not hypnotized by her gaze nor do we quote sonnets in the setting sun. Our enjoyment of each other's company has blossomed into a mature consideration I believe even you would admire. In fact, just yesterday we spent the afternoon on the Lower East Side. As a rule, I avoid such ramshackle neighborhoods, particularly in light of my being followed. But in this case, I had no idea what I was missing.

The coach refused to take us all the way into the dilapidated area so Mary led the way through streets shadowed by cheerless buildings listing from rotting beams. Curtains flapped through broken windows; dust swirled around our ankles; and discarded wrappers floated atop a stream of brown liquid as we wound among a tight labyrinth of peddlers selling live chickens and used trinkets from broken carts. Before I got my bearings, Mary turned at a corner showcasing a French bakery. Through a grimy storefront window, I saw a baker in a stained shirt rolling dough into flabby balls.

Mary had so far played coy about the purpose of our outing and the jostling crowd and rancid smells darkened my mood. When I stumbled over a plank lying on the walk, I felt a flash of hostility.

"Now that we're here, can you at least tell me why?" I asked. If my tone was brusque, Mary gave no indication. Instead she said hello to a woman scurrying past in a torn overcoat then stared ahead with a fixed intensity I found startling.

Mary explained she volunteered as an English tutor for struggling immigrants. She felt a calling to help those *tossed aside as used bathwater.*

"These brave people came here with hope and a desire to be part of something great, yet they are treated with disgust. We must do better, Thomas. A society is judged by their weakest, not their strongest," she said with a brief glance in my direction. I agreed in principal but kept my lack of firsthand involvement to myself. Had she looked my way again she would have seen my eyes cast to the ground.

We crossed the street and entered the mouth of a long narrow cul-de-sac. Except for a few scurrying cats, the road was empty. After the overfilled walks I should have delighted in the reprieve, but the sudden solitude had a disheartening effect. The tall buildings seemed to hunch over us, like the bereaved as the coffin is lowered, and distorted shadows from fire escapes made me think of a prison cell.

"We're helping a family who needs special attention," Mary said. I thought she would continue, but she kicked a rock down the center of the road and asked an odd question. She wanted to know if I had a fondness for children. I suffered a moment of panic and stammered. Mary shook her head.

"There's the most beautiful little girl you're going to meet and I just want to be sure you're comfortable. She'll need extra attention today."

My sigh made Mary grin. "Worried I was interested in talking about something else?" she asked.

"Indeed. Men have code for that kind of talk. *Time for a*

bigger carriage or *a second study might be useful.* We never actually speak the words."

Mary's chuckling echoed down the narrow corridor.

After assuring Mary I liked children, she pointed to the second floor of a large apartment house ahead. Our destination was a row of cracked wooden doors above a rusted staircase.

Climbing the stairs was slow, as we had to take care over missing steps. When we reached the landing, Mary took the satchel she had asked me to carry and slung it over her shoulder. She removed her black leather gloves and tucked them away. Then she unpinned her straw bonnet and used the thick navy ribbons to tie the hat to the outside of the bag. Mary then fished out a white muslin cap and put it on, careful to tuck in stray hairs.

Her preparations to teach English seemed a bit strange, but I chalked it up to cultural differences and asked if there was anything I should do. Mary shook her head and led me to the last door.

Mary tapped and a petite woman with pale features and dark hair opened the door. "Miss Mary. Vonderful. Vonderful." The women embraced and kissed each other's cheeks.

I was then introduced to Mary's English student, Mrs. Tzekernik. As I bowed, Mrs. Tzekernik grabbed my shoulders, kissed both of my cheeks, and gave me a thorough shake before setting me free and letting us in.

Piles of old clothing atop bare wood furniture cluttered the tiny room. In the dim light I saw a basin filled with grey water, a jagged round table covered with needles and thread, a potbelly stove leaking ash into the room, and a tan sheet strung from the ceiling. As it flapped back and forth, I saw another area with a mattress on the floor.

Across from the sparse kitchen was a narrow bed occupied by a young girl with ginger-colored pigtails. She sat propped up by a wad of rolled sheets and covered with a stained quilt. Though a bit pale, when she saw Mary, a bright smile plumped her cheeks and she tossed aside her book.

I learned Olenka was nine and learning English at a fantastic pace. Of late she stayed home from school, but Mary seemed confident she would soon rejoin her friends. "We can't keep those freckles away from the boys for too long," Mary teased.

Mary joined Mrs. Tzekernik in the kitchen and gave her a brisket wrapped in brown paper. Once again the woman seized Mary and hugged her. While the mother busied herself with the meat, Mary washed her hands in a basin by the stove then went to Olenka and sat beside her on the bed. She set her satchel by Olenka's feet and I waited for her to pull out a reader or perhaps some paper and pens. Expectations are often misleading.

Mrs. Tzekernik set a straight wooden kitchen chair beside Mary then went back to the kitchen. I sat and waited for an explanation.

"Miss Olenka, do you mind if I share what happened with Mr. Gadwell? Or perhaps you would rather tell him yourself," Mary said.

Olenka seemed eager for me to know her story but deferred to Mary for the retelling. As Mary spoke, the girl eyed me as one would a rabid dog. During my attempt to avert her stare, I noticed the girl's frail frame looked disproportional beneath the lumpy covers.

"Were you in Boston during the horrible blizzard last March?" Mary asked.

"The Great White Hurricane? Yes. It was horrific. I was trapped in the house with my father for three full days."

Regret struck as soon as the words left my mouth. I started to apologize, but Mary turned to me and said in a low voice, "I know you're nervous, Thomas. It's okay." Her compassion and intuition left me speechless, unfortunately not for long.

Mary continued. "It *was* a horrific storm and you remember how quickly the temperature dropped. New York instantly shut down. When it hit, our little miss was on her way home from school. She was extremely brave and found her way even through the blinding snow and frigid ice. When the storm passed everything seemed fine. But a few days later they noticed Olenka's foot was black."

"Frostbite," Olenka said. I cringed, but Mary assured me it was best to speak in facts.

"The frostbite was severe and required a doctor," Mary continued. "But doctors don't make calls here, where people are actually sick. They're too busy lunching till three and doting on debutantes with the sniffles." Mary took a slow breath. "Without a doctor there wasn't much they could do. Gangrene set in."

It took several seconds for me to realize what Mary was saying. By then Mary had Olenka's permission to pull back the quilt.

I jumped to my feet and blurted something about not getting in the way. Mary, however, needed my help and directed me to sit back down. I sat back down.

Olenka wore a russet wool nightgown that stopped just below her knees. Her pallid skin looked like bone china against the dark fabric. On her left foot was a man's baggy black sock; the right foot was missing.

The amputation was just above the ankle bone. Tight gauze wound around the end covering the stump, and as Mary inspected the bandage, I could see obvious seepage around the edges.

"We have to change the dressing today. I've brought some new medicine."

Mary arranged her supplies with confidence. There were several rolls of clean gauze, a spool of paper tape, a stack of cotton balls, and two small jars. One was filled with a clear liquid, the other with a paste. I steadied myself as Mary began to unwind the bandage. After just a couple turns, I again rose to my feet.

"I need to wash my hands," I said, lunging for the kitchen. In my haste, I tripped over the chair and toppled it. Snickering followed me to the kitchen. Then, since I was up, it was my job to bring back an empty tin to hold the soiled materials. I glanced at the front door in defeat.

When I returned, Mary had removed the old bandage. I held out the tin for Mary, trying not to stare, but the sight was a new experience for me. The skin around the stump had bruised and puckered where stitches closed the wound. I noticed a bit of dried green fluid but Mary told me it was ground herbs and not infectious pus. I again looked to the door.

Mary wet a cotton ball with alcohol and dabbed at the wound. Once used, she tossed it into the tin still in my grasp then asked me to prepare another one. I set the tin on the bed and did as she instructed. Mary also needed me to cut several strips of paper tape. I floundered until Olenka handed me a pair of scissors from the bedside table.

Inspired by Olenka's composure, my nerves settled and I became a passable assistant. I handed Mary salve and gauze on command, then when Mary finally re-wrapped the wound, she trusted me to hold the ends tight while she tied a knot. I did not flinch at touching the wound.

While Mary stacked the extra supplies on the table, I

cleaned up the used materials and took the tin to Mrs. Tzekernik. In a mix of stilted Polish, hand gestures, and simple English, Mary gave instructions to continue changing the dressing every day and said she was pleased with the progress and saw no signs of infection. Though I remained silent, I wondered if Mary was too optimistic. The stump looked a bit ragged.

With doctoring finished, Mary suggested Olenka take a nap while she worked with her mother. The girl looked to me, so I clasped her hand and said I would stay right by her side while she slept. Mrs. Tzekernik muttered something in Polish then whispered in Mary's ear. Mary blushed.

The English lesson was labored, yet Mary remained patient and tender as she corrected the young mother's backward letters and helped her pronounce a list of simple nouns. For over an hour they took turns reading aloud and reviewing basic numbers. The afternoon passed in an instant, so I was surprised to notice the fading light and cool breeze through the door. I checked my watch.

We were invited to stay for dinner and Mary accepted, hoping to have enough time to give Mr. Tzekernik his lesson. While Mrs. Tzekernik lit a fire in the stove, Mary pulled a bundle of carrots from her bag and held up a knife to me. "Everyone works here," she said. "Though based on your nimbleness I'm not sure you're safe with a knife." I prepared to defend my honor, when the girl awoke and begged me to play Old Maid. I held up my hands in submission. Mary huffed, but when she turned I saw her smiling.

After the game, Olenka taught me a Polish birthday song that sounded like "The Farmer in the Dell." Her mother joined in, and soon she and Mary were doing a high-stepping folk dance around the apartment. What a delight to watch Mary have so much fun. Then Mrs. Tzekernik grabbed my elbow and dragged me to my feet. Just as she swung me around, Mary's other student arrived.

Mr. Tzekernik is an enormous man with calloused hands and startling auburn hair. He served as a fishing boat captain in Poland but could only find work selling roasted chestnuts from a street cart and mucking the East End stable. As soon as he saw Mary he nodded and said, "Welcome." He then saw me, my arm still interlocked with his wife's, and he looked back to Mary. Mary nodded, and he held out his hand. "Welcome."

After checking on his daughter, Mr. Tzekernik stepped behind the curtain and returned with a thin book clasped against his powerful chest. Without any prompt, he sat at the table, opened the book, and began. Mary leaned close, seemingly unaware he smelled of sweat and grease, and listened as he read aloud. His pace labored, but from the pride on both of their faces it was as if he read a scientific journal instead of a child's reader.

Dinner was simple but well cooked, and with the help of Olenka's translations we talked about baseball. Everyone loves baseball.

The evening ended with hugs and Mrs. Tzekernik again kissed my cheeks. As we reached the door, Mr. Tzekernik slapped me on the back and said, "You are nice to Mary. She is *dobry.*"

Although not sure of the exact meaning, the message was clear enough. We shook hands before he escorted us as far as the stairwell.

The streets were deserted and most of the lamps were broken. Gusts of wind swirled loose trash around our feet, and in the distance I heard the sounds of fading cries and breaking glass. Mary took hold of my arm.

"I'm very proud of you, Thomas. You handled yourself well."

"Me? I was about to say the same of you. You'll make a terrific doctor."

Mary dismissed the idea with a shrug and shared again how much the amputation had healed. This was when I voiced my earlier concern, though in retrospect there are some details best kept.

"Trust me, Thomas, it looked much worse. There were no doctors, as I said, and the family doesn't have money for hospitals."

My heart seized. "Did the father have to—"

"The butcher. Did it in the slaughter room. At least he cleaned the knife. If it was during the war, he probably wouldn't have wiped off the cow blood first. We've learned a lot from the cleanliness of midwives. Still, it's taking a long time to heal properly."

"That poor girl."

"I'm blessed to know them. They are so very special," Mary whispered.

I squeezed her arm just as a man appeared from the shadows. He had a black hat pulled low over his eyes, and Mary tightened the grip on her handbag as he passed. Looking again at the isolation, I had a disturbing thought about Mary's travel arrangements.

Mr. Tzekernik walks Mary out of the neighborhood when he can, but she is not comfortable with an escort. She worries the families will think she is afraid of them. Her rationale was absurd, so I told her I could not permit her to travel without an escort. It was perhaps the wrong choice of words, but I stand by the sentiment. Mary replied she did not need my consent, and a quiet, but intense, argument ensued. She called the idea of a chaperone *nonsense;* I was shocked she was so stubborn about something so obvious.

When we had reached a stalemate, Mary flicked her chin forward. "Look, we're almost back. I see a few buggies and the street lamps are lit. This is hardly much of a walk. Please, Thomas, let's not talk about this now. I'm glad you worry about me, but I don't want this to ruin our day." Mary nudged my shoulder with hers. "You know, I think I may have a little competition. How do you feel about redheads?"

We concluded our evening without further incident, and overall it was an enlightening outing. Yet the following morning I was still agitated and again addressed the subject of her safety. My attempt to explain the realities of a harsh world soured by violence led to a passionate disagreement. Our heated quarrel swelled until it became obvious that these weeks of clandestine trysts have taken a toll on our nerves. In the end, Mary even revealed a deepening guilt from our secret outings. So, Henry, we have made a difficult decision.

After four glorious weeks it shall be excruciating to leave, but the time has come. We plan to continue our correspondence by means of Mary's dear friend, Miss Ross, who has agreed to act as messenger for our letters and keep Mary's confidence. However, the dubious fate of our courtship remains in the hands of a tyrant. Worse still, Mr. Harting's threat may not be so idle.

There is a chap in a charcoal coat. When I try to get a good look at him, he turns to peer in windows or raises a newspaper. Still, I am certain it is the same man because his right shoulder droops when he walks. Maybe I am paranoid, but I could not risk exposing my meetings with

Mary. Hoping to thwart any attempts to follow me, I have crisscrossed the city like a hound on a scent and began carrying a change of hat. I suppose this is another good reason for me to leave the city. My absence means Mary is in less danger—at least from the obvious thugs.

The industrious Mr. Kennard has graced the Harting household no less than five evenings these past few weeks. I must wonder what else he is stealing. It seems clear Mr. Harting is grooming Mr. Kennard for a place in the Harting family, my place to be exact, but his choice is peculiar. Mr. Kennard is of some importance to the company, but there is nothing obvious about his prime placement or thieving. I must figure out how to send him away.

My friend, I leave you here. Enjoy Edinburgh and your adoring Scottish fans. While you prove Yankee hacks can win a game of snooker, I must somehow find a fitting way to bid farewell to my dear love while dodging the man in the charcoal coat.

Regards,
Thomas

September 12, 1888.

DEAR AVERY—

Have you considered wearing a green felt Bollinger to the book signing gala? They are the trend in Milan and such a distinguished hat would suit your narrow face. Fashion tips and your attempt to motivate me by dangling another's success aside, I have news.

Hayes and his guards were most uncooperative and refused even to throw me a life preserver after my failed attempt to leap onto his private yacht. I had to dog-paddle to the dock using my pith helmet as a kickboard. Nevertheless, I am not heading home empty handed.

My train arrives late tomorrow evening. With me, I bring the nearly final pages of the second book and an idea for my third. You see, Avery, now I am ahead of schedule.

Thomas

September 14, 1888.

MY LOVE—

My despair is deep and unresolved. Our goodbye this evening was so awkward and filled with regret that I yearn to turn back the clock and do it again.

Our parting should have been memorable in a way that brings a secret smile, not this gnawing ache in my stomach. I felt certain that the boisterous group of men would leave, but they seemed intent on ruining our private moment outside the restaurant. Right then I should have taken your hand and led you to a quiet place, but the carriage driver was so impatient. My composure was shaken. I feel like a buffoon.

Had Cousin Penelope not accosted me as I walked through the door, frantic to share news of her engagement, I would have rushed to you without concern for your father's reaction. Sitting in Penelope's drawing room as she gushed about wedding plans was agony. After an hour, I pleaded exhaustion and returned to my room to write to you.

Although my impulse to rush to your door has softened, my breath is shallow and I am plagued with the image of your bewildered face when I mumbled something about a nice visit. *A nice visit?* Those are the words I shall say to Penelope when I leave, not what sums up my time with the woman I love.

I do love you, Mary Harting. Our time in California was brief; the smell of the salty air mixed with honey-glazed scones may have made me giddy, and it could be said with some conviction I charged forward like a stripling. But now I have discovered a real woman.

Should a man recite his reasons for love? Of course it would be easy to list your fine attributes and point to that as reason enough. But what would that prove? Were a man to skim the surface he would fall in love with a fairytale, an ideal that would soon enough shatter and scar.

I love you for your zealous opinions and impatience when you want to finish a task. You make impulsive decisions when provoked, and yet I have watched you brighten a room with your unguarded compassion and openness to new experiences. Your passion for kindness inspires, as does your heartfelt love of your family and good works. Perhaps in my vanity, I also love you because of your appreciation for my writing. At the hotel I did not even think to give you a copy of my first book, yet you quote dialogue and long passages from *Chancellor's Fate* with practiced ease. You are a magnificent woman and my affection for you is genuine. Regardless of your father's opposition, we shall continue our affair and wait with anticipation for the day we reap our reward.

Having released some of my burning emotions I'd hoped to feel better, but you should have heard these words whispered from my lips. Cold letters upon a page are a poor substitute, and you should call me a clod. I am a clod. I long to shout into the night, scream until my throat burns, but that would not ease what causes my hands to shake. Our parting must be replayed. I do what any man in my situation, and with my abilities, must:

Thomas and Mary stepped from the restaurant into the cool evening air. Though Thomas tried to lighten the mood, their last dinner together was stilted and Mary looked flushed from the café's bustle. Thomas watched Mary take a deep breath as she tied the thick sapphire ribbons on her bonnet. "Better?" he asked her.

She nodded, looked down, and then shook her head. When she lifted her chin, her cheeks were ashen. Thomas stepped forward, ready to sweep her into his arms, when a group of overindulgent young men rounded the street corner. Thomas took Mary's elbow and led her away from the commotion.

They strolled along a row of brownstones with scrubbed iron gates and trimmed potted ferns posed on small front porches. Reminders of the horses were cleared so the couple could smell the elm trees mixed with bread from an open kitchen window.

When Thomas spotted a community courtyard, he led Mary across the street. The gate was unlocked, so he pushed it open for her. Before she stepped through, she checked the street for observers.

Thick evergreen shrubs that had grown up the full height of the tall iron fence surrounded the courtyard. Golden light from the gas lamps gave only a muted glow, but Thomas could see a small rectangular yard with a lone elm surrounded by a patch of grass, a gravel path, and a small stone bench. He closed the gate with a heavy clang then heard Mary whisper his name.

"There's no one here to gossip about us," he assured her.

As she removed her bonnet, she turned and looked him in the eye. "Who said I was worried about gossip? Perhaps I find you too forward for a man on his way out of town."

"Perhaps, but I didn't push you through the gate. I certainly didn't hear any desire for a chaperone."

She stiffened and seemed ready to reply when Thomas wrapped his hand around her waist and pulled her toward him. He leaned forward and kissed her forehead. Her skin was warm and soft, and as he caressed her face she tilted her head and closed her eyes.

"Thomas," she whispered.

He kissed her cheek then let his lips slide down to kiss her neck. She smelled of lilac perfume and smoked meat from the restaurant. He tightened his grip on her waist, feeling the rigid corset and stiff crinoline pressed against her soft shape.

"Thomas, we shouldn't—"

He covered her lips and kissed her. She hesitated, and then they kissed as lovers in the shadowed light.

Mary broke their union and moved a few steps away. "I'm not sure even my sister would approve of this." She took a few quick breaths and sat on the corner of the stone bench.

Thomas paused, unsure what to say, until Mary turned into the light and he saw her teasing grin. He wanted to rush to her side and kiss her again.

"What time does your train leave in the morning?" Mary asked as Thomas sat down beside her.

"Too early for gentlemen, but I'll be ready by eight," he said.

"You'll be ready by seven so you have plenty of time to say goodbye to your cousin, Penelope. You'll miss her."

"That's not all I'll miss," Thomas said. He wanted to say more, but his pending departure hung like a brittle branch.

Mary faced Thomas and tightened her jaw. "So what happens now, once you . . . ?" She turned away and pulled a handkerchief from her purse.

"Leave?" Thomas put his hand on her shoulder, but she shrugged him away.

"I don't want to need you, Thomas Gadwell, and here I am blubbering over a man who actually believes Reverend Beecher was innocent of the adultery charges."

Thomas chuckled. "Is that the best you have?"

Mary caught her breath. "For now."

"You're beautiful."

She patted her eyes with her cloth. "That's hardly the point. Thomas, these past weeks have been unlike any time in my life. I can't believe I'm actually going to say this, but what will I do without you? I know that sounds ridiculous. I'm just going to miss you more than I know how to put into words."

"Darling, I promise we'll be together again soon. Your father just needs to give me a chance. It's strange; most people have to

know me better before they object to my liberal politics and boyish charm."

"I can believe that." She smirked then shook her head. "It's really unlike my father to act secretive and so blame . . ." She slapped her hand over her mouth.

Thomas laughed at her wide eyes. "You won't go to hell for saying 'blame.' "

"Or for sitting alone in a dark courtyard with a handsome man?"

"You think I'm handsome?"

"I think you missed my point," she said.

"So you say."

"I say," Mary snickered. "You really are silly sometimes."

"True. And you really are the most wonderful woman I've ever met. I'm in love with you, Mary Harting, completely in love with you."

Her laughter stopped, and Thomas swallowed against a lump in his throat. Though he had written it many times, hearing the words aloud made it more real. His voice sounded as if it belonged to someone else—someone more clever and deserving of loving such a woman.

She was silent, and he worried she did not want his declarations of love. He was leaving, putting down his sword and walking away. She had asked him to, but he wondered if it was too late to stay and fight. Thomas was ready to suggest just that, when Mary lifted her head. Fresh tears streamed down her face.

"I love you too, Thomas. I love you more than I ever thought it possible to love anyone."

She collapsed into his arms, and he felt her silent sobs against his chest.

"Everything will be all right. I promise."

Her tears turned to deep shuddered breaths, and when she lifted her head, Mary stared at him for a few moments. "You know your mother's right. You do have the mischievous eyes of an attorney."

"And what do you know about lawyers? Should I worry?"

She shook her head. "The only lawyers I know are old men with sagging bellies."

"Not handsome like me."

Mary tilted her head. "Who said you were handsome?"

He moved closer. "I believe a certain young lady mentioned my fine looks not minutes ago."

"Well, now you're just bragging," she said.

"Am I? So if I kissed you right now you wouldn't fall under the influence of my gifted appearance?" He leaned toward her, "And my wild charms?"

"Now I'm certain there was no mention of wild charms."

"Poetic license," he whispered.

They embraced in the quiet courtyard until Thomas noted the late hour. While Thomas checked the street, Mary replaced loose hairs that had escaped her chignon and put on her bonnet.

They went through the gate and stepped onto the sidewalk. The pavement felt callous and the air cooler than in the shelter of the thick shrubs. Unsure what to say, they walked together in silence.

The restaurant and street were quiet, so Thomas was disappointed when a hackney-coach appeared and stopped at his signal. He helped Mary into the carriage and shut the door.

"Mary, I know he'll change his mind. He just needs more time to accept the situation," Thomas said.

"I hate not knowing when I'll see you again. I don't like the unknown."

"Then you're missing the adventure, my love. Living is what we do between the expected and the mundane."

"A quote from your novel?"

"Not mine, but it's true just the same. I know it will all turn

out as it should."

Mary sighed. "Sometimes your optimism is maddening. Aren't you even a little bit afraid we'll never see each other again?"

Thomas shook his head with confidence. "We'll have a lifetime of courtyards, my love. I give you my word."

Mary nodded, but her lower lip quivered and fresh tears pooled in her eyes. Thomas winked and tapped the side of the buggy. He waved until the carriage disappeared around the corner.

The power of imagination is most curious, my love. If we replay this scenario again and again it will become as real as any memory. I intend to do just that.

Mary, we must endure and wait for your father's blessing. Until then, I will make a quick visit to Boston then head to Newport to start my third novel while your gracious friend, Miss Ross, delivers our words of life and love. Keep busy with your family and volunteer work. And above all else, my dearest, be careful.

With all my heart,
Thomas

September 17, 1888.

AVERY—

The train pulled into Boston a little past ten o'clock last evening, yet you denied me the pleasure of watching you streak across the window in your wool nightshirt and cap. Where were you? As my father is in rare form, we must meet right away. I plan to leave again without even a plate of pig's knuckles at Jake Wirth's.

T.G.

September 17, 1888.

DEAR BEAU—

Thank you for the unique evasion techniques and passionate warning about fish glue. Did you really have a yarn mustache stuck to your lips for three days? Now that I am back in Boston, I suspect I am unworthy of a shadow and will not need to "borrow" a barrel organ and monkey. I hope you gave them back to the organ grinder. Should I worry about you on foreign soil? Sometimes your antics get a little close to crossing the line of decorum.

Thomas

September 17, 1888.

DARLING—

The hall table is empty. I expected a letter with the afternoon post telling me how much you already miss my rambling tales. Have you forgotten me already?

Though my train arrived late, first thing this morning Father called me into his study to battle the merit of the Chinese Exclusion Treaty. Declaring my need for poached eggs and a good shave was insufficient. Since childhood I have despised everything about our infinite debates. It would be cleaner to draw pistols and have it done.

The torment begins when my father bellows for me from the base of the staircase. He has never found my company worthy of climbing the stairs. This is followed by loud, quick footsteps in the back hall. He wants to be sure I know he is waiting but he will not call for me again. The one time I ignored him, I was sent to bed without supper. I have never thought to ignore him as an adult. I suppose I would have to dine out.

As usual, Father waited for me in the doorway. My greeting met with his low grunt, followed by his pointing to the window. That is his way of saying it is time to take our positions.

My father propped himself against the corner of his Partners' desk with his arms folded and his face taut. The study smelled of the penny cigars he chews but never lights; newspapers he will not allow our girl to toss; leather bindings and withered parchment; and dust from the floor-to-ceiling bookshelves that line the room. As we inspected each other like ladies across a buffet table, I moved to the window and rested against the sill.

My usual manner is to pick up a glass bottle from Father's apothecary collection, something I can roll about in my hands to give the illusion of disinterest when I need time to formulate a rebuttal, but Father had cleared the display case. In defiance, I plucked my father's letter opener from his desk, held it before him with a grin, and waited for him to begin pacing. Unlike the rigidness of our dispositions, the mode of our debate depends on the time of year.

In the chill, we remain motionless, resting upon the marble fireplace while holding cups of steaming tea. When the weather is stifling, we open all of the windows and strut back and forth across the chintz rug searching for the right spot to declare our poignancy encouraged by a cooling breeze. In twenty-two years, we have never once availed ourselves of the leather chairs.

Our chat began with his usual rancor and belittling of my progressive ideas. Then, as he rationalized how forced labor does not violate civil liberties, I forgot myself and pulled a copy of *Surveying America* from the shelf. He stopped mid-sentence, huffed, and handed me a sterling silver marker the size of a berry fork. The library is littered with shiny reminders that one of their own is missing.

I took the marker and held it for a moment. "Please continue, Father. It's such fun to hear you degrade an entire class and dismiss common sense."

"That's not what . . . I . . . was . . . Thomas, just use the marker already. I don't want another book misplaced."

"For land's sake, I was seven years old."

We continued in this manner until my father checked his watch, stubbed his unlit cigar in the copper tin on the mantel, and walked out of the room indicating he was either hungry or tired. My dismissal, however, has never meant our discussion is over. Our vicious cycle shall repeat soon enough.

My father and this house were so distant when you and I were together, but I apologize for evading your questions. Not every family sings carols and plays The Checkered Game of Life. Now that I am submerged, I suppose it is easier to address your curiosity about my home life. Still, is it best you learn what else goes on behind velvet curtains?

Our residence at 84 Chestnut Street is a sturdy, four-story Second Empire with a boxy mansard roof, rounded cornices, and dormer windows that look like eyebrows. The front bay window is used to display Mother's needlepoint to the neighbors, and though my mother is fond of wishing it was as large as the Carnegie Mansion, our ten thousand square feet has all of the required rooms Mother has never decorated to her satisfaction.

We entertain with polished silver and china, ring our bell when ready for supper, and have the drapes aired each spring. When blue trellis wallpaper was stylish, we had blue trellis wallpaper in the front hall and receiving room, and my mother loves cherry wood and ivory trinkets. An attractive house, and yet I have not described our home.

In the summertime, we ate fried chicken on an old red blanket in the backyard and my mother always hummed unrecognizable tunes as she went up and down the staircase. I was never allowed to play in the guest rooms, and our cook, Lilly, loved to make chocolate bread pudding. The whole house smelled of chocolate—except, of course, on Sundays.

On Sunday evenings we always had a light supper then gathered in the family room. Father sat on the settee, his thick legs crushing the delicate rose pattern, and Mother put away her needle. From my spot on the floor, I watched Father stroke his mustache with a devious grin that made me laugh and shiver at the same time.

Father told stories. Sometimes he even acted out scenes and spoke in character voices like a performer in a company show. I never knew if his tales were original or borrowed from one of his many books, but it never mattered. We all looked forward to Sunday stories. Father even taunted us with cryptic hints during the week. But like the blue trellis wallpaper, story time was replaced, and Sunday nights were never the same.

Father had endless business meetings and missed church. He became hostile without provocation and began slamming his study door. He never discussed what happened with me, though Mother remembers the exact night when everything changed.

All the same, my childhood was not spent in misery. Lest I cast aspersions on a family you have yet to even meet, I shall move on to more pertinent information. It seems my few days in Boston are filled.

Upon my nightstand is an invitation to a garden party and Mother's sewing circle wants gossip from the West. However, speculating when and how we shall see each other again will occupy most of my time. I know you are eager to change your father's opinion of me, and your courage is admirable. But, Mary, you were so enthusiastic before I left. Please proceed with caution. Convincing your father to alter his judgment means he must first admit he is wrong. As this seems out of character, I fear the outcome of pressuring him.

Your loving,
Thomas

September 18, 1888.

MY FRIEND MALCOLM—

It must be at least a year since our last letters, and yet I recently told a special friend about our grand fort. Coincidence is indeed striking.

How wonderful to hear your discovery of medicinal uses for the Chilean blackberry was worth sleeping with a machete under your pillow. Although your interest in all things green is understandable given our experiences, when you fancied growing an assortment of complicated plants as a teen, I thought you just wanted to invite girls to your garden. Of course you did, but who knew then where your plotting would lead.

Your parents look well. We met at a garden party where your father promptly offered me another job. My response was quite clear. "No offense, sir, but I would rather go down with a burning ship than work in your factory again." He said my melodramatic decline was similar to yours.

By another strange twist of fate, I also saw our old neighbor, Samantha Mooring, now Jenkins. Do you recall taunting Samantha with a garter snake? I have no memory of such vicious behavior, but she described the event with traumatic detail. In fact, she was quite animated as she spoke about our friendship and sneaking through the bushes to spy on our fort. She even thought to inquire of your health but quickly added that your fine looks precluded her from ever giving you more than help with your philosophy assignments. Women are strange creatures, are they not? She intimated that gentlemen who turn a lady's head are not to be trusted. Having met her husband, he must be dependable indeed. Samantha also told me she ran into one of our old friends.

A little over a year ago, she accompanied her husband to

a dental conference in Worcester and saw William Crawley dining with a "bad egg." Samantha attempted to jog his memory, but William claimed he had no recollection of her and accused her of being a fussbudget. Could it be our jolly William is now a suspicious ruffian? I find it probable. The last time I saw William he was in a desperate situation.

Just before I started law classes, William stayed as our houseguest. You had already gone to the university and I was preparing to move into the dormitory when William showed up searching for a job in Boston. He never spoke of his need for an occupation, though based on a few offhand remarks, I believe the financial panic in '73 devastated his family. Our few brief conversations revolved around his disgust of Worcester and his desire for a lucrative position regardless of the type of work.

He would not speak of his parents, and I did not mention Gregory. He asked about you and if you were still a giant. For the record, you can no longer rest your elbow on his head. This pleased William, though overall he was distracted and agitated.

After just a few days, William left at dusk without even a note of thanks. My mother sent a letter to confirm his safety, and Father once mentioned he thought William went into banking. But it was quite plain our lives were heading down different paths, and I prefer to remember William as the boy who ate a grasshopper. Time indeed marches forward even though we are ill-prepared for the journey.

Malcolm, timing has met with distraction. It appears I was unaware of an engagement and the coach is waiting. I must apologize for this miserable excuse of a letter and bid you farewell. Once you finish your doctoral fellowship, you must come home for a visit. We will steal the yacht and take a long weekend.

Your first mate,
Thomas

September 19, 1888.

AVERY—

After months of your sending me pestering notes, hostile telegrams, and threat of a singing messenger, you have not yet replied to my earnest requests we meet. Are you using my notes to mop up spilled gin on your bedside table? Joking aside, missing previous deadlines hurt my income but never my career. Your silence is cause for apprehension. Is Harpers upset by my delay enough to pull the deal? I am well aware that Harpers's contract is not binding until the ink dries.

T. G.

September 19, 1888.

DEAREST MARY—

Learning you are well-occupied with a book fair at the Jackson Square Library gives me pleasure, and your suggestion the ladies settle the centerpiece dispute by thumb wrestling made me chuckle aloud. Also warm congratulations. New life is a true wonder, or at least my mother tells me she believed that before I was born. The first grandchild in your family is indeed a fortunate distraction for our letters. They shall notice your actions less the larger your sister shows.

After all day in a dusty parlor sharing anecdotes with Mother's friends and agreeing for sake of civility that bicycles are a sin to Crockett, my father surprised me by suggesting an outing. We went to The Meadows, a battered harness racetrack Father claims once ran thoroughbred champions and sold the best butter taffy. They no longer sell candy and most of the center rails are broken, but the temperature was pleasant and a refreshing breeze carried the stench of manure and echo of our fiery argument toward Salem.

My habit of gambling (rather my enjoyment as I would hate to give you the wrong impression) involves a pair of kings and a stack of chips. Father, however, has always fancied the trotters; his system of betting is more complex than his stock market speculation. After the thrill of winning in the fifth, we celebrated in the Turf Club with cold ale and the popular tradition of debating methods of capital punishment.

I believe the new technique of death by electrocution less humane than stoning a man. My opponent, a man suffering from a nagging cough and sore limbs for months, called me a ninny and retorted that all crimes should be punished as in the Good Book. This struck me as impractical, and for no particular reason other than it entered my head, I cited a sensational counterfeit scandal from ten years ago.

It was a fantastic bank scandal, and my father followed the news like a timekeeper at the factory gate. The counterfeiters were never caught, but if they were, I demanded to know how his rudimentary system of an "eye for an eye" would punish such a crime. Father was much more excitable than usual. He ranted for a full ten minutes about my inept debating skills before wasting his winnings on a nag named Papa's Dream.

Since our fun-filled outing, Father is irritable and depleted. His is unable to shake his cold and has begun taking afternoon naps. Mother and I, however, are joyous and at ease with each other; so much so, Father started growling at our incessant humming. As you have heard my singing voice, you understand his irritation.

Mary, by now you may have noticed my efforts to avoid the question in your last letter. If Mother's garden was showing a late bloom perhaps we could avoid this uncomfortable topic all together.

Rest assured, I attended the garden party with my parents. It was a laborious affair that required formal dress in spite of the unfortunate heat. Two ladies fainted. We left by six o'clock—before my aunt could present her list of available maidens and demand I make time for luncheons and, fingers crossed, romantic dinners. This was a definite relief, and yet you have broached a delicate subject.

Two years ago, perhaps a little longer, I met a young lady and we courted for a few months. You and I have not yet spoken of our romantic pasts; for me it is far easier to pen. I know you agree such matters are best aired and put away.

I pause, wondering if you would want to know her name. As a man, I prefer to think of your past callers as insignificant dolts with callous nicknames. Women, however, may favor knowing details so there is less to invent. It has been my experience women are far more creative in such matters. For this retelling I shall call her Gertrude, as this name is more fitting than the one given her at birth. Though I met Gertrude through my friend, Beauregard, his involvement in our attachment was quite accidental.

Gertrude was Beau's second cousin on his mother's side; in fact she still is. While not striking like you, it would hurt my own ego to claim she is monstrous. Most men say she is agreeable to the eye, with a fair mind and solid breeding that matches her complexion and figure. This may sound unflattering, but men are rather blunt when circling among their own.

We met at an informal dinner party at Beauregard's Cambridge home. Gertrude was pleasant, but I found her stories as dull as her sense of humor, and we spent most of the dinner chewing. You should now wonder why I pursued our association, since at first I had no interest in her whatsoever.

After dinner, the guests were gossiping about Leonard Jerome's naked carriage ride down Fifth Avenue over a glass of Tawny Port when Beau insisted Gertrude entertain us on the violin. My thoughts were on an early retreat, but the intimate party trudged into the music room with few expectations of finding entertainment except in the room itself.

A cascade of white silk hung on either side of two picture windows and white satin parlor chairs were grouped around a square Chickering piano. Deep walnut panels warmed the room and the ceiling was covered with a magnificent fresco depicting the Garden of Eden. It was striking, and the atmosphere would have been mythical if not for the intrusion of Gertrude's tangerine-colored dress.

Gertrude adjusted the strings and readied her bow with competence but without the gentility one expects from a musician. She stood beside the piano and proclaimed herself ready to begin. I chose a chair by the window so I could keep an eye on the weather, then Beauregard introduced her as if we were in Royal Albert Hall.

You know I am romantic at heart, my darling, so please remember my affections as I tell you more.

Until the moment she played I had never heard such magnificence with a bow. I was caressed by golden highlights that transformed the world into pure serenity and joy. The music was breathtaking and powerful, yet as vulnerable and precious as a new love. Dinner guests humoring their friend became grateful patrons. She ended the first section of Mozart's Violin Concerto No. 3, the Allegro, and we cheered, proclaiming she should have the first chair with the Boston symphony. She nodded with a slack expression, for her dull nature had returned, but I had witnessed something precious. Infatuated with her gift, I asked her to join me for lunch. Gertrude's mother was very formal and required a chaperone at all times. I hope you find this comforting. I did.

We met at the Union Oyster House on a dreary afternoon. Our lunch seemed endless, as Gertrude lacked curiosity and found single-word answers sufficient to my questions. She did not flirt or attempt clever comments, so by the time we got our chowder I felt certain the stewed clams were having a better time.

"This early rain is terrible for capes," she at last said after tasting the soup and making a sour face. "Long fringe is the style, but fringe will drag in the mud."

Unsure how to respond, I nodded and shoved a piece of sourdough in my mouth.

"Beauregard thinks I'm silly for worrying about such things, but then he's talking of an escapade to South America. Can you imagine? What could he want to see there? I hear it's filled with vermin and foreigners."

I chuckled, but her stern glance belayed any misconception she was joking.

"Yes . . . well . . . your violin playing is magnificent. I've never been as entranced as I was the other night. How long have you been playing?"

"My whole life." She sighed and pushed food around her plate.

Our lunch dragged on, and I was convinced it would be our only outing. However, as we were saying goodbye outside the restaurant I saw a hint of her cunning.

"I'm a member of a quintet and we're giving a small concert. We prefer to keep it personal. Only family and friends are invited. I'd very much like you to attend."

I agreed to escort her, and she smiled for the first time in my presence.

Before Gertrude, I would have never thought one's talent could transform everything about them. Based on the compliments and comments of others, I was not alone in my sentiment. It was magic, a bewitching magic that lingered long enough for another concert or intimate gathering where she promised to play a new piece or honor my requests. I knew her family well and her parents were fond of me. Before long the conversations turned to our future and prospective marriage.

To ease your mind, I did not propose. I have yet to propose to any woman. Even though I knew I was not in love with her, to say I never considered the idea is a lie. I was enthralled by her music and contemplated a life together. Henry set me straight.

The courtship ended without much discord. She had no deep feelings for me, and, upon our final conversation, professed she found my humor confusing. Beau and I are still friends and Gertrude married a pianist the following year. I have heard her play since our parting and am still in awe of her talent. I believe God shines through the gifts he bestows, even in the most implausible of hosts.

If this letter were addressed to Henry or Beauregard, I would not admit Gertrude was my only involvement beyond schoolboy infatuations. Once I began studying literature, my time was reserved for Chaucer, lacrosse, and the occasional gathering to sample spirits. Even today my writing requires months of quiet isolation. To have met you, my dearest, is a true miracle. I wonder how I survived all these years alone, but I can state with honest reflection I have never felt lonely until now.

Mary, I hope you find my candidness about Gertrude reassuring. When I was a boy, I asked my mother how a man could boast of courtships when ladies did not engage in such behavior. She was tickled, relayed my innocent question at least a dozen times, and told me I had better find a clever woman. She was quite wise. Still, I leave sharing the details of your romantic past to your discernment. It is well known young ladies with dazzling eyes rarely sit alone at parties. My true concern is with one specific gentleman caller of late.

While I create remorseful villains and reward the pious, life outside the pages of a book is unscripted and scoundrels often capture their prize. I never thought I was the jealous sort; however, you avoided any mention of Mr. Kennard whatsoever in your last letter. Before I leave for Newport tomorrow, I must ask: Have you spent more time with the industrious Mr. Kennard?

With love,
Thomas

September 20, 1888.

DEAR AVERY—

I am truly sorry. I know how hard you worked and accept full responsibility for Harpers retracting their offer. There is no way to hide my disappointment. If you can muster any more faith in me, perhaps you can send it to another publisher. In the morning I leave for Newport where I will plunge into my next book and nothing else.

With sincere apologies,
Thomas

September 20, 1888.

MARY—

Father collapsed. The doctor is here and Mother just sent for Father's attorney. I will write as soon as I can.

Love,
Thomas

September 25, 1888.
MY DARLING—
A man who once interrogated Ulysses S. Grant is unable to lift his head to sip from a glass of water. Doctor Stanton has eased some of Father's pain, yet over the past five days the good doctor has twice stayed all night and suggests we confirm Father's burial wishes.

My father suffered a heart attack during a small dinner party, collapsing just as the men gathered in his study to smoke dog rockets and tell bawdy jokes. He was so condescending at dinner, scoffing at my work and theorizing how I spent my time in Newport, that when he called out, I finished setting up the ladies' loom before going to the study. I was not one of the men who carried him to the bed where he now lies so motionless and puny.

Mother is extraordinary. She is composed and compassionate as she presses cold cloths to his forehead and changes his damp shirts. Though every Saturday my father set a white rose on Mother's breakfast plate, until I watched her kiss his brow I never thought of my parents as lovers.

Mother calls, so I must leave you here. Please pray for my father and that you and I may someday share such a strong bond. On such grim days it is difficult to imagine what will become of our future.

Thomas

September 27, 1888.

GOOD HENRY—

Do you remember the day I walked into your Beginning Fiction seminar and tripped over a chair? I suppose that would be hard to forget. Yours was my first class in anything other than law, and I had been tripping for days before I tore open my knee that morning.

After my stylish entrance, I headed to the back of Thayer Hall. You watched me, or at least it felt that way, and once I sat down you scribbled in a notebook. I imagined you were writing something horrible about how obvious it was that I had stumbled into the wrong lecture. Before I could scramble out of that class, you cleared your throat.

You pointed to me and demanded I stand and tell the class about my interest in creative writing. My limbs quivered so violently I feared everyone could see my terror through the hole in the knee of my trousers. As I stammered about a newfound creative passion, you yawned.

It would be most gratifying for both of us if I could remember your first lecture. I do recall the way your deep voice reverberated between the oak beams in the peaked ceiling, like a preacher in a well-built hall. The room smelled of mold and stale overcoats; the classmate behind me tapped his suede boot against my chair; and if anyone dropped a pencil you stopped and grumbled.

When for the next six classes you called on me to explain my literary pursuits, you must have noticed my confusion. I thought you were doddering. By the seventh class I had prepared notes for your inevitable question, but when you said my name I tossed them aside. My voice sounded coarse.

"You still want me to tell you why I'm here? I thought it was because I like to write, but that's obviously not what you want me to say. So here's something else. I had an internship at a South End law office where my job was to dig through stacks of files in a dusty back room looking for anything to absolve the back-stabbing, corporate swine known as the defendant. Well, I did just that. My discovery of an erroneous deed led to a dismissal. And what did I get for my diligent research? The defendant went on demoralizing his workers and I was handed a new pile of papers. I thought anything would be better, so I picked your class because of your fashionable pantaloons. Who knew suffering your lectures could be worse."

Remorse struck the instant I had finished, yet you responded by leading the class in a round of applause. Energized by my triumph, I cornered you after class. I still believe you only agreed to join me for coffee because you feared a crush of eager students if you stood in the hallway too long. Tell me, Henry, was I correct?

It seems comical now, but I strutted on the way to that overcrowded bistro with the stale muffins. It was cold outside and you hurried with your head toward the cement and your hands in your pockets. I had hoped to begin our discussion during that walk, but you never broke stride.

The drab eatery smelled of pickles and fried onions, and we were shown to a table that needed place settings and clean glasses. As soon as we sat down you rocked the table back and forth, grunted, then pulled a silver dollar from your pocket and stuck it under the short leg. Unlike professors who compared surnames with gold placards on the university's libraries, you looked me straight in the eye and asked what I wanted. I had such admiration for your writing. I found your approach refreshing. Now that I consider you my friend, I know that you just wanted to get back to work without suffering soggy hash or a soggy student. That, however, was not part of my agenda.

I desperately wanted to know if I had made the right decision, if my skills and motivation were sufficient for a literary career. Nevertheless, I had trouble finding the vocabulary for such a personal question and stammered like a lad facing the belt. You grumbled about the stupidity of convention then at last spoke. Your words still rattle in my head all these years later.

"I don't have answers that fit in a cigar box. I don't know if you'll succeed as a writer, and frankly I don't care. What you do with your life is up to you, not your father. It's your pine box." You plucked your silver dollar from under the table leg and walked out before I could even clear my throat.

If not for the invitation to Professor Reed's annual poker tournament where your losses paid for a month of rounds at the pub, I would never have overcome my awe to speak with you without frothy adulation and a facial tick. We are true friends, are we not? But it seems your role as mentor has yet to fade. Though I write this knowing there is little time for your guidance, Henry, I must again ask for your wisdom.

You once admitted you were unable to write even a brief note after your father died. Years later, do you still believe your work was silenced by what was left unresolved? Was it best you let him die without condemnation for the pain he caused you, or do you regret not airing your grievances?

My father is sallow beneath flushed cheeks and his breathing is labored. Last night I offered him laudanum for the pain, but he was overcome by a lifetime of regrets and pushed my hand away with surprising vigor. I begged him to wait for the reverend so we could preserve the fragments of our affection. Confessions are for clergymen ordained to cradle a troubled soul. Instead he forced me into a situation not meant for any son.

Along with a litany of business dealings Jay Gould would applaud, my father told me that he was mixed up in the '79 Worcester bank fraud. He admitted destroying evidence to help keep a friend of mine out of prison. I pressed him for a name, but his voice became too weak. Now I am left with the knowledge that my father is a criminal, as is one of my friends. What does one do with such knowledge, and how can a boy listen to his father's transgressions without passing judgment?

All I could think was that his admissions were insincere laced with the stench of death. Is it just that my anger is raw and consuming? Now I am saddled with keeping his lies and deceit, treacheries that involved a friend. My father is nothing more than the pretense of morality, and I was not the son of his prayers. As he withers and waits for his time on this earth to end, I pray God grants me the capacity to forgive him his weakness. As his righteous lectures ignite in my head like flash powder, this seems an impossible task.

Thomas

October 12, 1888.

SWEETHEART—

Your compassionate words of encouragement and faith have kept me from cursing God during these endless, sleepless nights. A few evenings ago, Father gasped for breath and his prominent chin slacked against his chest in a look of permanent resignation. Doctor Stanton left at sundown, packing away all of his vials and needles. After three weeks of prayer, we feared the worst.

Just before daybreak I left his side to fetch more water when Mother shouted for my return. Though I longed to slip away in the morning shadows, Mother needed my strength. I picked up the Bible and prepared to meet death.

I found Mother standing over him with her head bowed. Father lay still but his blanket was tousled so his bare feet were exposed to the brisk air. It seemed a dying man should have wool socks, thick black ones that rose above the calf. His feet looked just as they did when he padded across the dining room shouting for his slippers. I suppose I expected a dead man's toes to shrivel like dried blueberries. It was strange how his feet held my fascination, like a bystander gazing from the threshold. Just as I was about to cover them with the quilt, he wiggled his big toe.

We sent for the doctor at first light. Doctor Stanton took the liberty of bringing the reverend, so you can imagine his shock to find my father's heartbeat improved. Over the next two days Father's pulse strengthened. Several times he opened his eyes and winked at my mother before collapsing into a deep sleep. The cautious doctor attributed this to hallucinations. Yet, this morning Father woke with the sun and asked for broth—a good sign if ever I heard one.

Doctor Stanton warned of a long recovery, but despite

his caveat Mother is optimistic and insists I go to Newport. She has assumed full responsibility for Father's care and will not even discuss my continued help. So, my darling, I leave in the morning and shall get right to work even if my enthusiasm is a bit tempered by concern.

You are a most accommodating woman, Miss Harting, and your effort to raise my spirits in such a difficult time is appreciated. I adore the nickname, as Mr. Kennard does resemble a muskrat. That the Muskrat has dined with you several times and accompanied your family to the opera, however, gives me pause. Your finding him "dull as weeds" does not negate that another man watched candlelight dance across your soft complexion as he enjoyed your witty tales, and unless a complete idiot, is now smitten. The continued personal interaction with an employee is baffling and unsettling. Has your father given any reason for his interest in the Muskrat?

Your loving,
Thomas

October 12, 1888.

MR. GAYLORD, ESQUIRE—

Before you worry, Father is mending and there is no call to revise his will. I write with my own legal question of importance and urgency. My need is for a covert investigation into a man's reputation and past activities. Is this part of your repertoire?

Thomas M. Gadwell

WINTER 1888

October 15, 1888.

DARLING—

Do you recall your first time playing in the snow? My earliest memory is sitting beside Malcolm on a sled tied to the collar of his overgrown yellow Labrador Retriever. The previous summer the corner of our yard was tiered for mother's tulips; however, this was of no concern until we rounded the corner and found ourselves flung into the air. Before falling on my head, I remember thinking I might see an angel in the snow.

I still think of that day on mornings such as this. The air has turned; you can smell it, like the freshness of sheets as you slip into a chilled bed. It is the promise of winter, a reliable one to be sure, and like a good lad who has landed on his head too many times I wonder when I will see my angel.

Yesterday I arrived in Newport in fine health, if not spirits, after an arduous night on the steamer. The sea was in a foul mood and a light rain turned into an angry storm. I had wanted to begin outlining my next book but could not steady the gas lamp or my hand. Land was a welcome sight. Unfortunately, the heavy rain soaked my little hideaway.

All but the Newport market was closed when I arrived, though the market's colorful fruit baskets where I hid toads to frighten unsuspecting shoppers were tucked away. Each winter I am saddened by the island's drastic conversion from summer frolic—like a vivacious young girl pulling on a gray shawl. Newport is known as a summertime jewel.

In the warm months, fresh villas with vibrant green shutters dot the hillside, and gravel roads lead to marble mansions overlooking the sea. Ladies carry lace parasols and tie colorful ribbons around their necks. They crowd the streets to buy fresh cranberry tarts then eat their snack on benches facing the ocean. Errands are forgotten, and those in carriages stop in the road to gossip until Officer Henderson dispenses the traffic with a warning about strong winds along the cliff. I assure you he was not as polite about the frogs.

The true islanders are hospitable for profit. They have a keen sense of when to stock extra lemon cream for the mosquito season and will give directions to the Old Stone Mill for a modest tip. However, when summer ends the vacationers close up their retreats and the local men leave to take factory jobs in Providence.

The streets are deserted, the cobblestones are slack until the thaw, and the remaining shopkeepers lock their doors by two o'clock. Fog settles on the island like an uninvited houseguest, at times so thick it conceals the ocean, and a walk on the sand sounds like crossing a plank floor. The area is also partial to forceful gusts, sleet, and sudden, dangerous storms. For me the frost means isolation and forced concentration. True, when I sit by the window and watch strips of lightning explode through the clouds I miss the warmth and uncommon fellowship of summertime in Newport. Still, I thrive in the dreariness. I am not here to gossip in the streets.

Tomorrow I shall begin my sojourn into the creative

field of roses. At least this is where I hope to end up. It seems I have been lost in many other locations—the Bewildered Forest, the Pond of Stagnation, and from what I believe is too much time on holiday, the Coast of Trite. I can already feel the energy of my novel and am excited to get to work. And though my mother worries for my health, I have yet to find a better place to write than within the walls of Highflier.

Perched on a modest cliff, our family retreat is a grand specimen of a shingle style summer cottage with one of the broadest views of the Atlantic. Repulsed by the island fancy of gauze curtains which provide shelter neither from the sun nor neighbors, Mother spared no expense on sterling umbrella stands and leather upholstery. Nevertheless, I spend most of my time cloistered in one room.

Before long the library will smell of unwashed teacups, crumbs brushed from my desk, and crumpled sheets I pile in the corner. There is no use hiding such repulsive behavior and admit my habits so you can never claim I was a bottom dealer. Lest you worry for my health and hygiene, rest assured I shall encounter at least one person every day.

Mr. Fowler, property caretaker the last ten years, is the only winter staff. He is a curmudgeon who grumbles about housekeeping duties and lets the bushes cover the walk. When I arrived, I found Fowler in front of his bungalow singing "Amazing Grace" into an empty bottle of malt whiskey. His continued employment is a mystery. Nevertheless, unlike Father's ongoing tirade over luxury tax, discussion of Fowler's dismissal is taboo.

Though my hands tremble with anticipation to begin what I believe is my best story, Fowler has just brought round my horse. Soon I shall tell you about my idea for an adventure story set in your fair city, my heroine the handsome daughter of a wealthy railroad tycoon. Right now I must beg your pardon and leave to check on the neighboring estate. The mansion at the far end of the sea cliff has been vacant so long it was quite startling to see every room aglow. I shall take the rifle and alert Fowler to my destination. The dock master warned of robbers.

Your love,
Thomas

October 21, 1888.

DEAR MRS. WINCHESTER—

Thank you again for inviting me to stay for tea. After the dubious way our acquaintance began, you were most gracious.

Sincerely,
Thomas M. Gadwell

October 22, 1888.

AVERY—

I am already working. Never fear, my friend, this time the ferry did not drift off course and run aground in Bermuda.

Thomas

October 27, 1888.

MY DEAR MARY—

The book has begun with exhilaration, and I have again found my passion. My enthusiasm casts a long shadow, so I must beg your forgiveness for not writing sooner. You need not worry for me in a quiet house; imagination is fine company. And Mother writes that Father is mending well and she is in good spirits. Mary, I am more concerned about you.

To spend days folding napkins into Prince of Wales feathers deserves a footnote in the *Workwoman's Guide.* I have watched my mother oversee preparations for Thanksgiving dinner and often ask why she invites people she finds disagreeable, lazy, ignorant, and gullible. Her response is routine.

"Thomas, it's a blessing I gave you a passable face, because you're not at all funny."

As you said, at least sorting orange cups is more productive than quarreling with your father. Will you at least tell me what brought about such a harsh exchange? You relayed your profound guilt, though the details were so vague I suspect you were arguing about me. Rest assured, your apology will melt his anger. He knows you love and respect him even if you called him a "heartless beast." Your daring is proven, though I still advise taking small steps with your father. He is not a man you push into anything.

My darling, of course I understand why you want to go to Albany for Thanksgiving. As you enjoy a few weeks visiting with your sister and her husband, you must promise to imagine me brushing your knee under the dinner table. My plan was to endure Mother's wrath and remain here with cold turkey and a warm pen, but I have already accepted an unexpected invitation.

I am celebrating with my new neighbor, Mrs. Abigail Winchester. Though she was startled by my armed intrusion as she arranged glass beakers in a china cupboard (I was startled by glass beakers in a china cupboard), she appreciated my readiness to combat bandits and invited me for tea.

The parlor walls were washed with a pale stain giving them a feel of European antiquity, but formal portraits rested against the walls and the tea service sat on two moving crates. Except for a few servants, the aged woman is alone. She explained her husband died several years ago from what she called a "hunting accident." It seems his train derailed while traveling home after shooting a moose in Alaska. He survived the disaster but was then run down by a herd of fleeing elk. I stayed for a second cup.

She touted the virtues of naturalism though proclaimed a preference for staying indoors and addressed her girl in French. After the third request to remove the tea service, Mrs. Winchester snapped, "I said take it away."

The girl replied, "Sorry, ma'am, but I don't speak French. Begging your pardon, I told you that yesterday."

Mrs. Winchester huffed and said, "Yes, I know, but that shouldn't be my problem."

I expect Thanksgiving will be quite interesting.

Mary, I should return to my work. Distraction is my failing. I pray you enjoy visiting your sister even though our letters must wait for your return. Also, please ask Miss Ross to take more care. I see no reason for her to have delivered my last letter in your parlor. It is most critical your father is unaware of our correspondence. Are you certain he did not see my seal?

With love,
Thomas

November 12, 1888.

MARY—

Your last letter was delayed by the bumbling post. By now you have left for Albany, so I am left to stew.

With all due respect, was your father drunk when he made such an appalling request? He has again baffled me. Does he know his irrational and impetuous actions are potentially dangerous? Mary, you must refuse him at once.

Thomas

November 28, 1888.

DEAR ABIGAIL—

I feared my anecdote about mistaking Miss Astor's elaborate wig for a travel bonnet and asking to hang it in the cloak room was in poor taste until your psychic lost a full glass of Bordeaux through her nose. Thank you for an uncommon Thanksgiving. Also, I appreciate your assistance with my delicate situation.

Your acquaintance, Mr. Everett, sent a note stating his prowess in the practice of "private and discreet investigations." Though securing a referral for this type of personal research has proven difficult, do you stand by this man's reputation?

As it is too late to develop a musical talent and my clumsiness prevents me from performing card tricks, I caution that if I am again invited to your magnificent home the only entertainment I can offer is amusing tales.

With gratitude,

Thomas M. Gadwell

P.S.—Did your driver have an errand after the party? I was surprised to see another carriage on the road in the wee hours.

November 28, 1888.

DARLING MARY—

I know you are still at your sister's house, but I must write about Thanksgiving dinner before I forget even one fantastic detail. The outlandish folly was a welcomed distraction from dwelling on your father's preposterous demand. Still, I am beginning to wonder if your father's unpredictability is his most reliable quality.

Our hostess for dinner, Abigail Winchester, hails from Long Island, so I thought it curious she planned her holiday celebration away from home. I soon discovered the dinner party was not in good measure by Southampton standards. This, of course, made the evening even more enjoyable.

The night was brisk, but Winchester Manor (to which it is now referred) is a short jaunt so I ferried myself in the open coupé. I dressed without imagination in a black tailcoat tuxedo with a white bow tie and collar. My beaver-trimmed overcoat was comfortable, but during the ride I wished I had exchanged my top hat for a wool deerstalker. In fact, a flannel checkered hat paired with my black bib and tucker would have been better suited for the evening's nip and company.

While the estate has a gilded ballroom sought after by Mrs. Vanderbilt, the road to the house runs along a treacherous ledge hovering high above the sea. Wind swept up the bluff in furious bursts jerking the carriage from side to side. My steed's gait was erratic on the loose gravel, and twice he stopped and tried to back up. When I had at last reached the final turn, a strong gust pushed the tilbury toward the edge of the cliff. Fowler can make the minor repairs, but my father's lesson on taut wheel bolts has not left my mind.

My nerves more than a bit shaken, I arrived to find a

row of blazing torches and counted four carriages stowed in front of the house. As my feet touched the ground, a stable boy wearing leather leggings, moccasins, and a feather headband took my coach. The stressful journey was forgotten.

The house is styled after the Palace at Versailles in Paris, though Mrs. Winchester, who insisted I call her Abigail, may indeed have more bronze statuary in the gardens. Tall columns support an elaborate portico embellished with gilded winged cherubs, and two-story windows line the flat façade of the seventy-room estate.

True to the exaggerated architecture, I charged up a sweeping set of front steps and entered the colossal foyer through a fifteen-foot stained-glass door. The butler, an elderly man dressed in a dark coat and white gloves, took my top hat with what I later concluded was puzzlement, and directed me to the parlor.

I arrived last, a foible of some proportion as I was at least one libation behind. Then, when Mrs. Winchester greeted me dressed as a Quaker preparing to break bread with her new Indian friends, I feared I had misunderstood my invitation. But, indeed, the event was not a costume ball. My eccentric host was jovial and blunt about her love of costumes and eclectic gatherings to observe interesting subjects. As is just my luck, I was one of the evening's interesting subjects.

Mrs. Winchester wanted to know about my writing. She was curious where I found my ideas and how I could spend so many hours alone. For twenty minutes she prodded me, wanting to know if I included island gossip or chewed hallucinogens for inspiration. In exasperation, I told her authors sacrifice chickens to the gods of the press plate and bury the dead birds under a tree. The legend, of course, foretold that the larger the tree, the more readers. She squealed with delight, thought the sacrifice a marvelous idea, and insisted I conduct my next ceremony on her grounds. With Mrs. Winchester appeased, she made formal introductions. By and large, I struggle to associate new names and faces. I had no difficulty whatsoever.

First introduced was a Mr. Larimore, noted American flautist with the Belize symphony. Who knew Belize had a symphony? A bony man donned in a white tail coat and red striped vest, he never took off his white gloves for fear of injuring his hands. He had a silver tuning fork poked down through the slit reserved for a boutonnière, and he spoke in short bursts about the strain of living in such a warm climate and expressed scorn for American audiences. When he boasted Europeans were true music patrons, I asked his favorite concert hall abroad. He remarked he had not yet toured Europe and left me with his companion, a Belizean named Marianna.

Marianna, also a musician, was shy but told me she played the contrabassoon before blushing and returning to Mr. Larimore's side. Nevertheless, she had a pleasant, round face with large dark eyes that floated about the room and widened every time she looked at Madam Rousseau.

A self-proclaimed spiritualist and reader of Asian tiles, Madam Rousseau was swathed in a gold ruffled gown. Around her neck she wore a gigantic purple amethyst she claimed cured chronic back pain and boils. The thick black cord was so tight, her fleshy neck and cheeks were vermeil. Before being properly introduced, Madam Rousseau strode up to me, poked me in the stomach, and said, "You're a mysterious and reclusive young man. There's an indigo glow around your manhood." At this point I begged for a glass of whiskey.

As I took my first sip, I met two men in matching violet morning coats and paisley bowties. Jarrod and Theo (they would not disclose their last names) were businessmen from Atlanta who used phrases like "crooked as a dog's hind leg," guzzled ale from a jug, and burst into song whenever the impulse struck.

I felt stiff and out of sorts in my black regalia until I met Miss Katya Petrova, a budding opera singer from Russia. For the evening she chose a modest emerald tea gown with a beaded collar and matching feather pinned in her piled hair. I found her pleasant, but as she spoke little English, she spent the evening grinning, which I felt compelled to return. This grew quite tiresome.

The standard dinner fare was lavish and well served, although our host barked orders to her servants and found fault with the texture of the bread pudding. I found it rather smooth, but Madam Rousseau coughed a great deal during this course and Mrs. Winchester assumed she was choking on pieces of bread rather than acknowledge the Madam's rather tall glass of rum.

I found a receptive audience for sharing a few of my short stories, in the broadest of outline of course, and was invited to vacation on the coast of Belize any time between the fourth and tenth of June. After dinner we were entertained with an aria from Beethoven's Fidelio accompanied by the flute and contrabassoon, a rare and unauthorized rendition to say the least, and I concurred that with training and promotion, Miss Petrova might gain a fine reputation. However, the highlight of the evening was still to come.

Madam Rousseau, who regaled us with tales of psychic mysteries I shall someday include in a work of fiction, plucked me from the sofa and asked me to join her at the dining table. I obliged, but not before a wisecrack about also living to regret breaking plates over my head at a festival in Corfu. She muttered under her breath, a voodoo curse by the look on her face, and the entire party hurried to the dining room so she could read my tiles.

We sat across from each other at the cleared table like gamblers ready to draw, and then she pulled a gold tin from her flowing gown. She presented it to the group just as Genovese salesmen display diamond keepsakes to eager American shoppers. I must tell you, my dear, it took great restraint not to ask where on earth she kept that tin.

She removed the lid and emptied ten thick ivory tiles onto the table. A few tiles were colorful, but she turned them face down before I could see their design and slid them on the smooth oak. As she mixed the pieces, she closed her eyes and swayed back and forth. It appeared as if her head was ready to fall off and roll to where we had just carved the turkey. Then without warning, her eyes popped open and she said, "Pick three to reveal your future."

I shrugged and reached for the closest, but she slapped my hand and cried, "You dare to touch the tiles!" Her voice was so shrill Theo spilled wine on Jarrod's jacket.

"The spirits are close. I can feel them," she continued. "You must think of what you most desire, what you want deeply." She grabbed my hands and pulled me forward until our noses almost touched. "But you must think of only one desire," she whispered. "If you choose more than one you will curse your entire family."

As she breathed on me I realized the spirits were indeed close.

I pointed to three tiles because it would have been rude to laugh and ask for a second piece of pumpkin pie. She nodded and turned them over. Mrs. Winchester gasped, but I found their design rather intricate and smiled as Mrs. Winchester bit her index finger.

Darling, have you ever seen Asian tiles? They were a new experience for me. What I saw looked like a mix of Mahjong and domino tiles accented with common eastern images. Madam Rousseau was silent as she studied the tiles, and I later overheard Mrs. Winchester tell Jarrod that ghosts required silence to communicate. I believe Madam Rousseau needed time to invent what she was going to say and was jealous at the speed with which she composed a gripping story.

Mary, I hope you are not alarmed by her fortune. Though Madam Rousseau may have hunches like my mother, the idea she can see the future is as silly as her necklace.

"You're in love," she declared. "You're the prowling tiger and the red dots symbolize a strong, fertile heart."

"Thomas, you devilish boy," Mrs. Winchester blurted.

Madam Rousseau ignored the interruption. "But you are torn between two loves. The tiger sits between two ladies, pulled in opposite directions. See the cherry blossoms. They mean you will soon face a dilemma that will cause great misery. We must see what will become of this."

She paused and looked at me as if I was to do something, but I waited, not wanting my hand slapped again. She turned over a fourth tile—a green dragon.

"Death," she shouted.

This time Jarrod spilled wine on my jacket.

"You must choose one love or both will perish. Do it quickly, or you will lose everything."

She slumped into her chair and claimed the spirits were gone and she was exhausted. Recovering from such strenuous activity required a large glass of bourbon and several pieces of Belgian chocolates.

Mrs. Winchester was delighted and thought the best way to uncover my deep secret was to pester me until I broke like a wild colt. Of course I repeated that I did not have two loves and that the Madam was just excited after a large meal. To this, Madam Rousseau called out "poppycock" and fell asleep on the settee.

The evening concluded well into the morning hours, but as I made my retreat down the front steps Theo tapped my shoulder and mumbled something about my writing. Before I could beg off to go home, his eyes rolled up and he slumped to the ground. I shouted for help, to which Jarrod and Mrs. Winchester strolled from the house. Mrs. Winchester poked Theo's bottom with the flat front of her pilgrim boot and pronounced he was asleep. This was when I heard snoring. I left to Mrs. Winchester and Jarrod singing "I Know a Youth Who Loves a Maid" as they dragged Theo into the house.

Mrs. Winchester insists I make time for tea and has extended an open invitation to visit. Although she is quite sturdy for a woman in her seventies, it is imprudent to keep such a large home open during months of unpredictable weather. I shall keep an eye on her.

Seems fodder abounds even in the most implausible setting. Lest you worry about my validity, I spoke the truth when I said I am not torn between two loves. I am in love with one extraordinary woman, and that is enough for any man. Hopefully we can soon flaunt our affection in front of witnesses. Until that glorious time, my concerns are more tangible than idiotic predictions.

Your father's actions are suspicious. Has he ever before demanded you accompany him on a business trip? I must wonder if his desire for your company is to keep you under his watchful eye. Mary, I am concerned he knows about our letters.

Your devoted,

Thomas

P.S.—I received your telegram before sealing this letter. Staying with your sister for Christmas is a wonderful change of plans. But why is it imperative you return home for New Year's?

December 18, 1888.

FOWLER—

Cigarette wrappers have collected by the stable door. Father may tolerate your idleness, but I expect a property caretaker to care for the entire property. This includes dusting the guest rooms and sweeping out the stables. Must I again remind you of your duties? And when did you take up smoking?

Thomas

January 1, 1889.

DEAR AVERY—

The new year brings promise and redemption. My resolution is that you will not be disappointed in me, nor me in myself. While I imagine you indulged in the usual festivities, I spent my New Year's curled up with what I hope you will soon agree is a good book.

Thomas

January 4, 1889.

DEAR HENRY—

Do you love writing your first drafts as much as I? All of my rough drafts are masterpieces until I read them. However, based on the short story you enclosed, your drafts really are works of genius. Did I like it? That you are asking my opinion reminds me how far we have come since you christened my early prose. I am pleased you no longer consider my writing drivel and am honored to reply as a colleague, a friend. Your story is stunning. It is the high-point of the collection. Your brilliance also underscores the inadequacy of my antagonist, though my excuse is undeniably colorful. Since opening a fresh calendar, my reality is more like your fiction.

For starters, Mary's father wants to drag her to a city once called the "bloodiest town in the West." This is more than unorthodox, Henry, it could be dangerous. Even a bookish fellow like you must have heard of the infamous Abilene, Kansas.

I remember sitting with my mates passing around sketches of Abilene saloon girls. Even as a boy I understood Abilene was a lawless, drunken sprawl ruled by armed cowboys and the cattle trade. We, of course, wanted to visit. But why in the world would a loving father risk taking his daughter to such a place? And what sort of dealings require that Mr. Harting trek to Abilene in the worst of winter? As I start to unravel this new development, another is in knots.

My father's solicitor was insulted by my request and would not provide a reference for a detective. Fortunately, I met a woman with the splendid combination of eccentricity and affiliations; however, I have yet to decide if Mrs. Winchester is a whimsical gentlewoman or offbeat harridan. After full exposure to her collection of dead spiders in specimen jars, she believed my rather chilling story about searching for a lost friend last seen in the opium dens of San Diego and provided a reliable referral.

I have hired a Mr. Everett to handle the delicate research of Mr. Lowell Kennard, the antagonist in my plot. Thus far I have been encouraged and shocked by Mr. Everett's enthusiasm. Tidbits of interesting information are in my custody, and some are quite suspicious for a man looking for suspects.

As I studied the preliminary dossier last night, a full glass of cognac warming in my palm, I was ill at ease. I have no claim against Kennard so great I should know the amount of his income (impressive) or that he saw a physician for a purple rash. My ego is certainly robust. Nevertheless, I was unable to stop reading.

Mr. Kennard started at Harting Railways as a junior payroll clerk. After just two years, Mr. Harting promoted Kennard to Vice President of Development. Why would he promote an inexperienced man to such a high rank? Also, Kennard made a big show of telling Mary about his philanthropic work for the downtrodden. He even spoke of organizing a charity ball with a guest list to rival Carnegie's annual Memorial Day picnic. It might interest Mary to know the bilker has considerable investments in dilapidated tenements and makes a considerable profit on inflated rents.

Mr. Everett has not yet ascertained Mr. Kennard's birthplace or childhood records but is confident his roots are not in the state of New York. Kennard never made any specific claims; still, he led me to believe he was a native. Does he want everyone to suppose he hails from New York because his background is less than desirable? Of course, I am reading more than what is written on the page but shall continue with vim. At least I was relieved Kennard's rash was not typhus.

Mr. Everett's next report is expected soon, and a criminal profile is also available, provided I am interested and generous. This begs the question why Kennard has a criminal profile. Maybe he is just a kleptomaniac caught pinching carnations for his lapel, or maybe he is involved in something more dangerous. I am ill at ease, my friend, ill at ease.

Thomas

January 5, 1889.

HENRY—

Amazing what can change in just one day. Yesterday I had one worry. Today my distress is doubled. It feels like one more turn of the screw.

This morning I trotted into town for something other than rotting potatoes and canned corn. Mrs. Potter, owner of Pelican's Cove, gave me her annual bear hug then led me to a seat by the window. My mind was on cakes and eggs, so when Mrs. Potter leaned against the table and began asking questions, I was a little confused. Once I sorted it out, I was dumfounded.

She was most curious to know if I enjoyed visiting with my old college roommate. His coming to see me was a secret, she said, and she was dying to know if I was surprised. Henry, you may remember Beauregard was my roommate. Beau is in Greece.

Mrs. Potter left to fetch salt for the corner booth, so I looked around the room trying to imagine where my mystery "pal" sat and if he ordered the clam chowder or lobster bisque. I jumped when Mrs. Potter returned with a plate of buckwheat cakes and scrambled eggs.

"So how come you never told me you spent a year in Europe and played lacrosse in college? And I didn't know your mother's from Albany. I have a cousin in Albany," Mrs. Potter paused to wipe her forehead with her apron. "So is your friend one of those animal doctors? He knew a pot full about trolleys and horses. Told me most hackneys are in better shape than private carriages."

A shiver ran down my spine, and I pushed my plate aside.

The questioning continued in this manner, to which I created an occupation, heritage, and political affiliation for my friend. Then I learned Mrs. Potter and her fourteen-year-old daughter spent an hour sharing all they knew about me with the stranger. I had no idea they knew so much about my habits. They left out only my shoe size.

Henry, what if Mary's father actually sent his henchman? Do people do that? I never confirmed my being followed in New York and, until now, cast it aside as paranoia. But what if the man in the charcoal coat was one of Mr. Harting's many eyes? I must be rational. Even if someone is watching there is nothing much to see. My days are spent huddled in my study, and from now on I will keep watch when I post letters to Mary. Whatever comes of this, I must admit this stranger's knowledge of my background is unnerving. Perhaps Mr. Everett is not the only detective snooping around.

Thomas

January 6, 1889.

MARY—

The hour is late. I am huddled under the blue afghan my mother crocheted as a gift for a friend but never wrapped because she thought she dropped too many stitches. She warned what is imperfect is flawed, and what is flawed is unfinished. So I blame my mother for the pile of torn pages in the corner, the plate I smashed against the sideboard, and a frightened messenger who shall think twice before again knocking on my door.

Tonight I have rested and waited for a moment when I can address my concerns like the man you met in California and not the one who needs a good shave. My time in contemplation has welled mounting fears about you accompanying your father to a cow town infamous for ladybirds and the Chisholm Trail. Your assurance the gambling halls and brothels moved north with the cattle trade was not at all amusing. Even if the area is now as quiet as your father claims, dragging a young lady on a grueling business trip in the midst of winter is, to say the least, dubious. Even you admit this trip is queer and uncivilized. What will you do for two months in Kansas?

Surely your mother is upset and will worry for your well-being without proper society or a companion to tour the area. Does your father expect you to spend your time trapped in your hotel room or shall he take you to tour the stalls? Yes, you may indeed have time to convey my fine qualities and exceptional breeding to your father, like those of a purebred bulldog, but what if you are unable to find a sympathetic inn keeper to deliver our letters? I doubt your father's discovery of our conspiratorial exchange would win me a blue ribbon. On the contrary, his knowledge of our continued courtship could cause considerable harm.

Must you always obey your father's commands? Mary, I remind you of your adulthood. You can refuse his request and deal with the consequences. On many occasions, like your going to the gala, I prefer you do just that. I state with bluster that I loathe the generous details you included about the Muskrat's New Year's Eve party. Solitude is not always best for an imaginative man.

You forget I have indulged in extravagant society balls and can envision the bounty of four-in-hand drivers alleging dry throats for reason to whisper in a girl's ear. I can see you with your hair swept in a low knot, dancing and laughing with every eligible gentleman with able vision and fair health. Even though your father insisted, you did not have to so enjoy the party. I would expect the Muskrat's duties as host and masher kept him quite busy. Did you in fact spend much of the evening with Mr. Kennard?

True, the Alliance Literary Program shall make great use of his charitable donation; nonetheless, his motives are most obvious and less than altruistic. I feel it within my rights to abhor such an open display for your attention. At least if you must go to Abilene, and it seems you are packed, you will have time away from Mr. Kennard and his charity balls. This is a thin but strong vein of encouragement.

Mary, my tone is like rotting milk thistle for a reason I have yet to share, though I take nothing away from my previous disgruntlements and would like to keep my distrust of the Muskrat and disapproval of your upcoming voyage on the record. When I was in New York, Cousin Penelope spoke of a June garden wedding, but I just found out Mr. Lancaster must go to England on extended business so the wedding is now set for the end of February. While you are traipsing through Abilene cow fields, I will be in New York.

This is maddening. Penelope's wedding was to be our grand unveiling. You were to sit beside my father so the two of you could chat about politics then dance the Jenny Lind. Mother would ask how we met and you would charm her with descriptions of the hotel and snicker at the extra bit of bourbon in the mint juleps. Circumstance again shoves our affection into a gulch. How long can we fight to reach sunlight?

The last log has fallen from the grate. Smoke and ash sting my eyes and the windows groan from the wind. My mood has not improved, though I had few expectations of that tonight. I am out of sorts and admit some of my unpleasantness is stirred by desires a man can never slake with words on a page. Nevertheless, I respect your commitment to changing your father's opinion of me, even if I believe your tactics are misguided. My prayer is that this trip affords what you expect. Before you leave, I ask only that you stay away from the Muskrat. I believe he is conniving and not the least bit motivated by helping underprivileged immigrants.

Remember, muskrats are pests that do their destructive burrowing under cover of nightfall. They are crafty, wild creatures that live in bogs and swamps. Killing a muskrat requires a cage and sharp axe. I have both.

Yours,
Thomas

January 11, 1889.

DEAR MOTHER—

Thank you for warning a long letter is keeping Father from using your Parisian handkerchiefs to clean his hunting rifles. I promise to reply—if just to save your handkerchiefs.

How long have you suspected my interest in a young lady? Was I that obvious? Seems I have again underestimated your intuition. Her name is Mary, and yes, she enjoys working in the garden. My intention was never to keep her from you, in fact quite the opposite. But her father is a disagreeable man who finds me repugnant. Mary believes she can change her father's opinion by badgering him. I disagree and provided solid rationale for my opinion. Mother, can you interpret her last letter? I thought Mary would appreciate my sincerity and concern for her safety. Instead she is fuming.

Thomas, you are so preoccupied with work and other interludes that perhaps in your consumed state you have forgotten that a girl living under her father's roof does not discuss or disobey.

Why? What would her father do? Moreover, what does Mary believe he would do?

And besides, do you really think my father would take me to Abilene if it were unsafe? He may be many things, but he loves me and wouldn't do anything to hurt me. And even if the area is a tad rough, you know full well I can handle myself. Your constant worrying is offensive . . .

How could she possibly take offense to my concern? Would she rather I not care at all?

and I find your sarcasm—I hope it was just sarcasm—offensive. I want an apology.

Yes, I will apologize.

I honestly thought you would thank me for my commitment to changing my father's opinion of you. Surely you can see the benefit of my spending time alone with him. There is nothing to do on the long train ride but talk. I can make him understand what we mean to each other. You must concede this trip can be used to our advantage.

I can, and yet I could never forgive myself if she were harmed on my account.

I share your disappointment about the wedding and was also looking forward to meeting your parents, but I will not just sit around and wait . . .

Is that a subtle criticism?

. . . for our situation to change. I must, and will, do something. And, by the by, it was your suggestion I keep myself busy while you are consumed by your passion for work. The gala was a fundraiser . . .

She spent a very lavish evening in the company of another man.

. . . and I spent most of my time encouraging patrons. Yes, I did spend some of the time with Mr. Kennard and he was a fine gentleman. My glass was never empty nor was I left alone in the corner. These are merely facts and are not meant to allude to anything.

Then why tell me at all? She should have kept the details unless I asked.

I will not speak any more about Mr. Kennard. But I will say one more thing about this trip with my father. With or without your blessing, I am going to Abilene. I will convince my father of your exceptional breeding and fine character even if that means trotting out your qualities as a show dog and overlooking your threat of axes . . .

It was more of a suggestion.

and cages. Really, Thomas, was that necessary?

My letter was perhaps a bit coarse, but I explained my grievances with clarity and stand by my sound reasoning. Even so, I know you will tell me an apology is in order. I think it will be more believable if you could shed light on *why* I should apologize. Sometimes we all need another perspective.

Your loving son,
Thomas

February 1, 1889.

FOWLER—

Your incompetence is intolerable! While hurrying to Winchester Manor the rear axle clip snapped clean in half and the carriage catapulted. If not for the good fortune of a large log, I would have careened off the cliff and plummeted to my death. Are you trying to kill me!

February 2, 1889.

MR. EVERETT—

I am indeed interested in what you "stumbled upon" with regard to Mr. Harting. Also, where is the criminal file on Mr. Kennard? Recent circumstances dictate urgency. I shall be in New York on personal business in a few weeks and would like to arrange a meeting. I expect you are gathering information at full chisel and have much to share.

Thomas M. Gadwell

February 2, 1889.

DEAR HENRY—

Paranoia has returned and this time with tangible reason. Has your carriage axle clip ever broken in two? Has anyone's? I assure you a ridge-top ledge is a horrific place for a suspicious malfunction. This accident, combined with my inquisitive "college roommate" and Fowler's insistence he has not taken up smoking, despite evidence to the contrary, means I can no longer swallow my nagging concerns.

Though unfathomable outside the pages of one of your stories, I must consider Mr. Harting's threat and the possibility he has discovered our letters. Still, Doyle's new Sherlock Holmes would not jump to conclusions. Given Mr. Kennard's desire to sit at the Hartings' dinner table, perhaps the Muskrat is shrewder than I imagined and has discovered Mr. Everett. For now the doors are locked and my panic is growing. I welcome your counsel.

Your esteeming,
Thomas

February 8, 1889.

MY DEAREST—

Your resourcefulness in engaging a young embroidery student as messenger was inspired. I just hope you are not miffed by my actions as I awaited word of your safe arrival. Upon my request, the editor of the Abilene Chronicle sent some fascinating back issues. I have not read such obscure prose since Henry's class on seventeenth-century essays.

Did you know Abilene cowboys herded over three thousand head of cattle each summer? This is impressive for a one-horse town run by hooligans living in clay shacks. Wild Bill Hickok served as marshal until he accidentally shot his friend, and a group of drunkards once tore down the jailhouse with their bare hands. Then the cattle yards closed, and the town crumbled. Today they grow some wheat and mourn a dead economy. So naturally, Abilene is the perfect locale for a winter holiday.

Your description of vacant, bullet-riddled buildings and weeds growing in the streets is dismal. Though the town is not the wild village I imagined, I still worry for your constitution in such a depressed area. My concern for your welfare, however, does not mean I underestimate your abilities. You are indeed capable of taking care of yourself. Men simply desire to protect their loved ones, and my inability to shield you is more frustrating than you realize.

Also, please accept my apologies for comments against your father. I was discourteous to you and your family and now understand young ladies have few liberties while living in their parents' home. Of late I received some wise guidance. It was not my intent to add to your burdens with my hostile and suspicious mood. My actions were unfair. Still, Mary, I must encourage discretion when delivering mail to your embroidery student. I believe your father is watching. Please be careful.

Once you have set photos on the nightstand, I pray you will share more than a few thin comments on the atmosphere and weather. Mary, you seem despondent. Your pen is labored; the thickness of the ink betrays your contemplation and the deep creases tell of a letter that was opened and closed many times before it was sealed. When you are ready, I ask you tell me what weighs your heart. Darling, what you can never hide from a man of words are the ones that are missing.

With loving concern,
Thomas

February 21, 1889.

MY LOVE—

My work is sometimes consuming and days run on like too many of my sentences. Can you forgive me for not writing in almost two weeks? I was trying to finish another chapter before leaving the island and time slipped away. That you have written only a few brief notes about the comfortable inn eases my guilt but not my worry. Are you unable to hide your letters or are there other troubles you wish to conceal? My prayer is that your father realized his mistake and you are on a train heading home.

I had planned to slip away to Penelope's wedding without incident, but Mrs. Winchester insisted I join her for a send-off dinner. Though she dressed like a pirate (complete with an eye patch and sword) and commented I should marry before I have jowls, she has a wonderful cook and interesting company.

We were joined for dinner by Miss Katya Petrova, the Russian opera singer I met at Thanksgiving. Mrs. Winchester has taken a personal interest in the girl; I dare say Mrs. Winchester has supported all of her music lessons since arriving in this country. After a passionate aria, Miss Petrova demonstrated her developing skills on the piano. The moment her fingers touched the keys, I thought of you.

She played the score you played on our last afternoon at the hotel. I felt the damp breeze from the open window and the chords vibrated off the polished oak in the empty ballroom. The memory of how I longed to kiss your cheeks and take your hands in mine was so clear it took Mrs. Winchester's abrupt shove to startle me from my daydream. I regret Miss Petrova misinterpreted my distraction.

The poor girl became nervous and quiet before retiring

earlier than Mrs. Winchester expected. As I was putting on my gloves, Mrs. Winchester plodded toward me and I prepared for a lecture to rival my grandmother's sermon on civility. Instead, she asked a peculiar question.

She wanted to know if I were acquainted with you. In my surprise, I blurted meeting you and your family in California but said nothing of conviction. She dismissed me without further inquiry or my usual plate of blueberry muffins for breakfast. Have you forgotten to mention your family's acquaintance with Mrs. Winchester?

My ferry to New York leaves tomorrow morning. Though uplifted by a reprieve from the island's shadows, thinking of Penelope's wedding stirs memories I wish forgotten. The ceremony has developed into a grand affair with at least three hundred guests, and according to my mother, that many doves. I was corralled into serving as usher, and Penelope just wrote to ask if I would make the final toast. She was reluctant to impose but declared "only my talent with words will keep the evening from turning into a total and utter shambles."

I have attended many weddings but been asked to participate just once before. It was during a time I call the "lost year," a boundless chapter in my life I often wish I could go back and edit. Truth be told, I regret my arrogance even more today than I did eight years ago. Meeting you has opened my eyes to the impetuous young man I was. Though I have never shared this painful event with anyone, I feel compelled to share my dishonorable behavior with you. Few secrets are kept well for long.

Right after college graduation, as I planned to start my first novel, Beauregard appeared on my doorstep. He had a smirk that bragged he was up to mischief, and in retrospect I should have closed the door. Instead, I invited him to dinner with my parents.

Confining himself to pleasantries and flattery, Beau waited until Father sliced the roast beef and set the carving knife on the sideboard before announcing the purpose of his call.

"If I may, Marcus . . . Mr. Gadwell, sir, I came here tonight to ask if you will allow Thomas to accompany me to Europe. We shall begin in Paris." He turned to my mother and added, "Where we will not see such finely twisted hair." Looking back to my father he continued, "Then we will tour the French countryside, meet with society in London, and explore the Swiss Alps. My interest is in paying homage to historical cathedrals and visiting my third cousin in Lisbon. I expect such an extensive and educational trip might take up to a year, but as you know, Mr. Gadwell, that's the standard these days."

Of course I understood full disclosure of our escapade would commence over a lager at the pub.

"You should go, Thomas. Travel broadens the mind. Your mind could use some broadening," my father said. His quick agreement was such a shock that Beau muttered something a bit vulgar and spent the next five minutes apologizing to my mother.

Just one week later I stood at the dock shaking hands with my father. Mother was too upset to see us off. She feared I would marry a French coquette and never return home. Father wished me a safe journey and added, "When you've tempered your wilds you'll be ready to get back into law."

The next month we enjoyed a grand time of endless festivities. We indulged in rich wines and company, and had yet to even leave Paris. When the weather cooled, we headed south and moved about the extravagant ports of

Nice, Cannes, and Monaco—our stops dictated more by amiable girls than our tickets.

When Beau lost a tidy sum at baccarat, we departed Monte Carlo for Rome and vowed to enrich our minds by exploring the sights. As respectable lads touring Italy we made acquaintances with fellow Americans renting apartments for the winter and often secured invitations to evening gatherings in crowded parlors. We were not discriminating and indeed met striking characters. Someday I will tell you about our wager with a bullfighter from Madrid. I still use his banderilla as a letter opener. During one such evening, the parlor busting with extravagant velvet costumes and exotic accents, Beauregard met Francesca Ferrara.

Francesca was someone's niece visiting from Sicily, though I never met an aunt. She wore her long black hair pulled behind her ears with loose strands down her back. A tall woman with a slim physique and oval green eyes under thick dark eyebrows, there was something fluid about the way Francesca curtsied to the Americans and fluttered her unadorned fan as she gazed around the room. Beauregard was captivated. Although Francesca had but a meager mastery of English, she knew French well enough for them to chat for three hours that first night.

For the next two weeks Beau stayed out every night past midnight. When he returned to our room, he tossed his top hat on my stomach to wake me up and babbled about Francesca. I had never seen him so enthralled. Then one morning he woke me at dawn. It was Sunday. The bell from the Basilica San Clemente was announcing daybreak when Beauregard began shaking my shoulder.

"Wake up, you coot. I'm getting married," he said.

It was either the shocking news or wet washcloth Beauregard slapped against my face, but I jumped up. In the process I knocked over the bedside table and stubbed my toe.

"What?" I asked, holding my foot.

"I'm getting married." He had already put on his charcoal morning coat and pinstriped trousers.

"To whom?" I blurted.

"Get dressed, Thomas. We have to hurry. That means you don't have time to decide between a kerchief and that ridiculously tall Piccadilly collar. A tip, my friend, little boys all around the world are begging not to wear their Piccadilly collars." He plucked the pillow from his bed and thumped me on the head. "Now, pull foot. I'll meet you downstairs."

He rushed out the door before I could ask any questions, and I remained startled for a few moments. Not knowing what else to do, I dressed and met him in the lobby.

"My God, Thomas, what took you so long?" Beauregard waited by the bell desk. He examined me like a woman choosing a frock and said, "Good. I can see your neck. That's a start. Francesca thought you were an altar boy."

I asked again what was going on. "I've already told you," Beau replied. "I'm getting married. Francesca is meeting us in a little village outside the city. The concierge is getting us a carriage, and you're my best man. What more do you need to know?"

"I need to know if you've lost your crackers."

It was not warm congratulations, I admit, but I was too flabbergasted to search for a more tactful approach. I do believe Beauregard felt hurt by my flippant comment, but he punched my shoulder and led me to the carriage.

"Will you at least tell me how all of this happened?" I asked.

"Thomas, my innocent young friend, how do any two people fall in love? It just happens. I asked her last night and she said yes. That's all there is to it."

The carriage driver opened the door so I was forced to pause long enough to take my seat and watch Beauregard give the driver directions and a handsome tip.

As the carriage lunged forward I said, "Of course that's not all there is to it." I was vexed by his cavalier attitude. "Beauregard, you've only just met. Surely you need to know more about her. You haven't even asked her father for her hand. What if her family wants you to live in Sicily? Are you going to live in Sicily? Beau, there's a thousand questions. You can't rush into something this important."

"Take a deep breath, Tom. I'm the one that's supposed to be jumpy. Funny, but I don't feel nervous." He slid down the window and slapped the side of the carriage. "Isn't it a handsome day?"

"You never call me Tom."

Beauregard shrugged then gazed out the window and whistled an odd tune. In a rather confounded state, I had so many questions my head began to pound. The most pressing question was how Francesca arranged a wedding on the fly.

Beauregard shrugged again. "I don't know. Francesca knows the parish priest at a little Catholic chapel named . . ." he paused, "well, dash, now I can't remember the name of the chapel. But it's in the center of town with a nice view of the lake, and Francesca was sure the priest would marry us today."

"How does she happen to know of a village chapel? For heaven's sake, Beauregard, you're not even Catholic."

He bragged how Francesca traveled a great deal and knew the area well. "And so what if I'm not Catholic. He can legally marry us, can't he?"

A disturbing thought entered my mind. Beauregard once said he admired Francesca's modest style, how he had grown tired of women using the illusion of French perfumes and diamond tiaras. I said he was daft, but his words were forefront in my mind.

"Beauregard, does she know of your inheritance?"

His silence confirmed I had overstepped my bounds, and I wanted to apologize when Beauregard turned from the window. His merry smile had faded.

"Thomas, you sound just like your father."

I reacted just as he intended. We were young, driven by rash emotions and at that moment I was too insulted to speak. We stared at each other in silence then Beauregard turned away and continued looking out the window. The tension in the carriage rose until I was glad when we at last arrived and found the church. Beauregard tumbled out of the carriage and rushed inside. I refused to follow and sulked outside.

We were perched on a rise surrounded by lush farms I had failed to notice while brooding in the carriage. There was indeed a breathtaking view of an azure lake and a quaint chapel with terracotta walls and a listing bell tower. Beside the chapel was a graveyard. A narrow gate held together with chicken wire scuffed across the soft dirt, and crumbling stone markers were laden with fresh dandelions. The chapel and cemetery reminded me of dear old chums who had exaggerated tales of their youth and complained of a chill in June. As I thought about Beau and the importance of our friendship, the bell rang releasing bits of rust into the breeze.

Beauregard bounded out the chapel door. His eyes were wide and he snapped his head back and forth between me and the road. "She's not here yet. The second service begins in a few minutes and she's not here. Where is she?"

I then noticed a few wagons and assumed the parishioners were already inside. "Oh, my very young friend, you should know that blushing brides have a great deal to primp and fluff and who knows what. You can't rush these things," I said, then winked.

Beau grabbed my shoulders and hugged me. "Thanks, Thomas. I knew you of all people would understand. You're a foolish romantic at heart."

"And you're just a—"

"Don't say it. I want us to stay friends."

We chuckled, and I told him to go inside while I waited for Francesca. "You're getting married without anyone's approval and in a language you don't understand. You could at least follow one of the rules of matrimony."

He looked at me with a blank stare, so I waited for him to state the obvious. Instead he rolled his eyes and said, "Sakes alive, just tell me what you mean. My head feels like I'm wearing your stupid collar."

"The groom's not supposed to see the bride before the wedding, you ninny."

He slapped his forehead and agreed to go inside. Before he left, he made me promise I would let him know the moment she arrived. I saluted, and he trotted back into the church.

A few minutes later a cab rounded the corner and pulled up in front of the chapel. I waved off the driver and helped Francesca from the carriage. She was dressed in a simple white tea gown with small pink flowers on the crown of her head. Though she wore no jewelry or veil, a little surprising for a young bride on her wedding day, I found myself in agreement with Beauregard. Her simplicity was elegant and fitting for a country ceremony.

"Good morning."

"*Buon giorno.* Is here Beauregard?"

I was about to reassure her he was inside panting like an overheated dog when the breeze caught the edge of her dress. As she collected her long skirt she dropped her colorful bouquet so I bent to pick it up. This was when I saw the heels of her shoes. If not for my close examination no one would have ever noticed. I handed her the flowers and she nodded, unaware of what had just happened. The church bell rang again, and she took a step toward the door.

"I'm sorry, Francesca, but Beauregard isn't here. He's made a mistake."

"Miz take?"

I nodded, unsure if she understood, until she lowered her bouquet. I asked if I could do anything, knowing I had done enough, but she stared at me and said nothing. I attempted to ask in French, but my pronunciation was hopeless. Francesca touched my arm and shook her head. She got back into the carriage, and I watched her leave.

I intended to find Beauregard but instead leaned on the cemetery fence and listened to the worshippers sing "Angus Dei." When Beauregard found me I could not bring myself to tell him what I had done. We waited by the cemetery for a full hour. He was confused, angry, and then remorseful, but he never suggested we search for Francesca. I still believe this was because Beauregard knew it was for the best.

We went back to the hotel, packed our bags, and I offered to go anywhere he fancied. Beau would not agree to shorten our trip and go home, so we continued on to Austria and Switzerland. In time we took up our rounds of social calls and late nights, but we were both more subdued and Beau was distracted. Our trip went about in this manner for the rest of the full year and Beauregard did not mention Francesca until we were aboard the Isthmus sailing for Boston.

"Thomas, how did you know? You were right all along. She only wanted to marry me for my money," he said to my question of how he was enjoying his filet. "I told her all about my father's company, my holdings, and even bragged we could travel the world on my enormous allowance. What I don't understand is why she changed her mind. I guess she decided money wasn't enough to make her happy."

He was quiet a moment then mumbled, "Dollymop."

"Beau, that's a bit harsh. She wasn't—"

"I want to think of her as a dollymop or strumpet, but I can't because I still love her. She probably only wanted my money and I still love her. I'm a darn fool, Thomas. You tried to warn me, but I would have socked you if you had said anything else in that carriage." He tossed down his fork and pushed away his plate. "How long will it take? How long until I don't think about her every minute?"

All I could do was shake my head.

Had I not seen the careful application of white paint she had used to conceal the shabbiness of her shoes they would have married. I made a grand assumption she lusted only for his property and that Francesca was just another of Beau's passing infatuations. I wanted to protect his future. It was brash and egotistical, and I curse my arrogant youth. What if theirs was true love? I may have ruined his life.

Cousin Penelope's wedding brings up many painful emotions. Though I wish to share in Penelope's happiness,

I resent leaving my work and cringe at the thought of New York without you. Most of all, I detest writing a special toast to love and the vows of marriage for someone else.

Though jealousy taints my pen, I will not disappoint Penelope. I ask you to judge if my "talent with words will keep the evening from turning into a total and utter shambles." You are truly the only person with whom I long to share this sentiment.

A man walks his path with purpose until he is distracted by a rose-scented breeze. He has found his way though he never knew he was lost.

A woman steps through her gate, dreaming of the road ahead. She is cautious but moves forward with optimism.

Two paths cross and the man and woman move as one. Unexpected and divine, the excitement of life begins.

To the happy couple.

Thomas

February 22, 1889.

DEAR BEAU—

Are you enjoying your escape from the arduous occupation of finding amusing society and resting from afternoon strolls? If you can pull yourself away from the beauty of the Greek climate and inhabitants, I should like to see you when you return. After you entertain me with a sensational narrative that ends with you not changing your shirt for three days, I have much to confess.

Your friend,
Thomas

March 5, 1889.

MR. EVERETT—

Your incompetence is intolerable. Knowing Mr. Kennard was jailed in Omaha for three days then released without charge does not ease my fears. What I want to know is why he was arrested. Your claim the police report is sealed is outlandish. You forget my background in law. Only presidents have their records sealed. And as for your startling information about Mr. Harting, I am well aware of his associations with racketeers.

Had I the time, I would already know more about Mr. Kennard, including his whereabouts before moving to New York. Mr. Kennard did not materialize as a ghost. You will not extort any more money for information already promised. I demand you fulfill your contract.

T. Gadwell

March 5, 1889.

FATHER—

I will not apologize to your man Fowler. That you are blind to his incompetent caretaking must be another convenient effect of the laudanum.–T.

March 5, 1889.

MARY—

I returned from the wedding elated to see your delicate script, yet I was accosted the moment I opened your letter. I would like to know which of your friends wrote such slanderous gossip. You know full well I did not escort anyone to Penelope's wedding. You have no right to claim me insincere and untrustworthy, nor do you have any foundation for rebuking alleged actions. While I share my love and concern, you report on the eiderdown pillows. *You* are angry with *me*?

In case you care to learn the facts before accusing me of being a libertine, my arranged dinner companion was not on my arm the entire evening and is a cousin I have not seen since childhood.

The idea you think my love is some kind of game is preposterous. If that were true, I should hope I could find better amusement than dealing with a family who finds me beneath contempt without reason. I dare say, most parents consider me a desirable suitor. I am an eligible gentleman of means with a reputable family and full head of hair.

And what do you believe of my work? You carried on as if I spend my time cavorting and sipping champagne because I sometimes dine with my elderly neighbor. Most days I am sequestered with only the sounds of my scratching pen. My nights are long and often sleepless; I dine on burnt roast and stale bread; and my only company is the lushington in a stupor on my study floor. When I venture to the market, I am cornered by saps eager to know if I am done with my next masterpiece. It has been four months, so of course I must have finished by now. How easy it is to write. How entertaining and simple; they should also take it up as a hobby so they can afford an extra girl in the summer.

The warmth in this friendless winter is your letters, and now that is tainted. Must I wonder what irrational feminine hysterics await me because I was seen in the company of another woman? What does it matter? I am a cad, "an insincere lech using my fancy words to woo every woman in town." Think what you will and do what you must. For now I am too busy wooing every woman in town!

March 6, 1889.

DEAR HENRY—

As soon as I arrived back in Newport I felt as if someone were watching me. I have not seen anyone yet but am unable to shake the feeling I am back in harm's way. Then again, after the last row with my father I would rather face a scalawag. I took your good advice to make amends with my father now he is recovered. My father has healed well; back to his old self I would say. My mistake was assuming a mere brush with death would change him.

After the wedding, I knocked on my parents' suite and Mother showed me into the sitting room. Her needlepoint canvas was on the floor.

"I need to speak with Father. Is he awake?"

"Yes, but he's not accepting visitors."

I threw my gloves on the coffee table. "I'm not a visitor."

"Keep your voice down. Of course you're not a visitor," she said. "That's not what I meant. He's in a fine pucker, Thomas. You know how he gets. Why don't you leave him a note before—?"

"A note? This isn't something to write in a note. Mother, I have to speak to him."

She looked out the window to the bustling street below. "You know how I feel about the grief between you and your father, but you need to give him more time. Go and work on your wonderful book. He'll send his letter when he's ready."

"Yes . . . well . . . I'm ready now." I plucked the top hat from my head, dropped it beside my gloves, and strode into the bedroom.

My father rested in bed, his torso propped up on a thick pile of pillows against the carved oak headboard. His face was far from the sunken frame when I had last seen him lying in a bed. He had on a fresh nightshirt, his hair was combed, and his thick mustache was trimmed. In fact he looked a little tanned and was smiling at something amusing in the newspaper on his lap.

I strode into his room a man, not the boy I become when we are alone in his study. He looked up but did not put down his newspaper. I motioned toward the chair by the window.

"You can sit as long as we don't discuss my health. I'm sick of talking about my heart. I'm fine."

I agreed to his stipulation. I had no intention of discussing his health.

"Thomas, did you hear there's property for sale in Turtle Bay? It might be an opportunity for residential redevelopment," he said.

"I'm not here to discuss the New York housing market. Father, we need to talk about what you confessed. I must know which friend was mixed up in the banking scandal and why you destroyed counterfeiting evidence to help the guilty party escape justice. You're culpable. We can't just leave things like this."

He folded his newspaper and put his hand to his temple. "My head hurts, Thomas. Go get your mother."

"What?"

"You heard me. I need some of my medication."

I stood up, the boy returned for that brief moment, but then I sat back down. "Which is it, Father? Are you too ill to admit the truth or do you feel fine? You can't have it both ways. I won't allow—"

"You won't allow?" He crumpled his newspaper. "Who do you think you're speaking to, young man?"

For the first time I felt indifference to his blazing offense. He could shout if he wanted, but I no longer cared; I needed to understand. I insisted we could not go on as if nothing happened.

He turned until his black eyes settled upon my unwavering stare. "I don't know what you're talking about. I don't remember much of anything while I was sick. Doctor Stanton says laudanum clouds the mind. I don't remember telling you anything about a scandal."

I pleaded for him to stop, but he continued the charade, "Thomas, I really don't know what you're talking about. There's nothing to discuss."

"Yes, there is. You must tell me who—"

"I said there's nothing to discuss. Now leave me alone. Go to Newport and pretend to work while I actually—"

"Father, we—"

Through clenched teeth he spat, "I said leave me alone."

I left the following morning.

Seems reconciliation is improbable. At least while on the lookout for a dodgy henchman, I also have an angry lover. You of course know the latter is the most dangerous.

With reverence,

Thomas

March 9, 1889.

DARLING—

Your apology came before I could finish my own without revealing my foolishness. My pen was driven by irrational, frustrated wrath, and the ugliness of my letter hovers like the California fog that dampened the deck chairs. Can you forgive me? I have read and reread your letter with a heavy heart for all that you are feeling. My talent for candor pales in comparison to yours, but I must at least try.

I still believe my leaving New York was a good decision, but now knowing you felt abandoned makes me ashamed. You feel I left without trying to fight your father for you, and I must agree. Though we based our decision on sound reasoning, there is another important reason why I agreed to our parting with such ease. You should know the truth.

My dear, I left in large part because I needed to begin my book. In truth, I wanted to begin my book. I know I vowed our courtship would continue unfettered, but I was wearing blinders and had forgotten that writing is an endless struggle without a victor. My schedule is odd and self-serving, and until now the consequence has hurt only me and Avery. It was never my intention to neglect you, and still I must acknowledge my preoccupation. The man you met at the hotel wants to stroke your hair and whisper he will change his ways; the writer at this desk will not deny his passion nor regret the time it demands. Perhaps Madam Rousseau was in fact correct about my two loves. Change, however, first requires desire.

My feet are not bound to this island. Yet just as pride prevented you from asking me to stay, ego prevents me from returning. My affection for you has not faltered as you fear. It grows without measure even though a selfish will controls me. Darling, if we are ever to succeed in our attachment you must understand writing is all I have to give this world. There are too many that expect failure and belittle my efforts in hope of breaking my spirit. I will not satisfy them. Can you forgive me my temperament? Men are so different from women. Seems you have learned even a loving father is just a man.

I understand your disappointment and wish there was something I could say to cheer you. Yes, it appears your father took you to Abilene because he never trusted us and wanted you under his watchful eye far away from me. At least his protectiveness has kept you from the Muskrat. This brings me more reassurance than I can explain. However, now that you concede there may be nothing that will change your father's mind, we must stop and consider this reality.

In the pages of a manuscript the protagonist must reach a point of vulnerable exposure. His destiny rests in that moment of conflict, yet he is brave and resolute. Never in my life have I felt less heroic than right now. This is the most distasteful of anything I have ever had to do; however, the question must be asked and answered. I think we both know the time has come.

My sweetest Mary, are you willing to build a life with me if our union means separation from your family?

With all my heart,
Thomas

March 21, 1889.

HENRY—

The winter frost in Newport is cutting yet I shiver from more than the driving sleet that pelts my chin. I wish my fear was from the finished chapters stacked too close to the fire. But I fear more than my pages are in danger.

After returning from dinner with my neighbor, Mrs. Winchester, I went around to the back porch. My habit is to use the rear entrance closer to the study. This infuriates my mother who writes to remind me that, as a gentleman, I should use my two capable limbs to go to the front. I had just put my key in the lock when I heard footsteps behind me. Before I could turn, a man grabbed me and shoved me against the door.

"Gadwell, I've been waiting too long for this," he said as he pressed his full weight against me. I squirmed, but he was twice my size and he had my right arm pinned to my side while my left was twisted up against my back. He spat the cigarette from his teeth and ashes flicked on my cheek.

"He said you'd struggle. Waste of time."

"Who said? Mr. Harting?" I asked.

"I don't know names. What I do know is the boss wants you to stop what you're doing. He don't like it." He pressed harder. It felt as if my arm might snap in two.

"What don't the boss like, your breath?"

"A wiseacre," he said. Then he jammed his knee in my back. Sharp pain shot through my side and down my legs. "You're lucky this is just a warning, you boot-licker. It's your last one. You got that, Gadwell? Next time I won't be so nice."

He grabbed a fist of my hair and slammed my forehead against the door frame. As I sunk to the ground, I heard him leap from the porch and trot into the night.

I crawled inside and slept on the downstairs sofa clutching my father's old rifle. The next morning, I reported the incident. Other than a blinding headache and aching arm, proof of my tale is just a small cut over my left eyebrow. Seems my head is thick from years of bad reviews. A few greenbacks persuaded the police sergeant to patrol my street, but I jump at every creak and wasted a whole afternoon sighting targets. The henchman has nothing to fear.

Can I accuse Mr. Harting without evidence? Should I terminate my contract with Mr. Everett even when we have unfinished business? Above it all, I was likely attacked for a reason that no longer exists.

Twelve days ago I asked Mary to decide our fate but she is silent. Can I blame her? While she needed me to whisk her away into the sunshine, I buried myself in work. She is disappointed, which I fear is much worse than anger. So now I wait for Mary's answer like a dying soldier watching his blood stain the innocent meadow. I should refrain from mentioning blood. It reminds me I must also figure out what to do before I no longer have two capable limbs for entering round the front of the house.

Thomas

March 24, 1889.

MR. EVERETT—

Upon further reflection, I am unable to keep treading water while you splash along the shore. Though my experiences are not as broad as the ones you claim for yourself, I have had my share of calluses and am unafraid of getting my shirt dirty.

In stopping to lay out the pieces of this puzzle, I was reminded of my thirteenth year, when I spent two summers at Weston Shoes. The company is owned by my good friend's father, and they made, and still make, quality leather boots. Employment was arranged to instill an appreciation for hard work. I instead learned the definition of piercing the corporate veil and saw what happens to a man betrayed by someone he trusted.

Weston Shoes once advertised consistent leather coloration and so dried and cured their own leather. The tanyard took up the back of the factory, and as it was considered the lowest level of work, I was to start as a trimmer. My position, however, changed in a single breath.

During one of the many times you dodged bullets, blocked knife attacks, or outwitted police captains, did you happen upon a tanyard? Chemical vapors and dusting powders created the look of a misty day by the sea. Upon first sight, my eyes burned. When I stopped in front of two men using large brushes to apply a white powder to pale hides strung on lines, I found it hard to breathe.

As the foreman began explaining the process of drying the leather, he stopped mid-sentence and asked if I was well. I wanted to say I felt flushed, but my throat was so tight nothing came out. I tried to breathe but could muster just a short gasp. One of the men brushing powder dropped his bucket and hurried toward us. "Can't you see he's reacting to the talc!" he shouted.

The foreman grabbed my arm, shoved me back through the door, and dragged me to a stairwell where he deposited me on the bottom step to fetch me a glass of water. Within seconds my hands swelled and broke out in red bumps. The allergy was so severe I could not even withstand the talc residue on the leather.

That foreman's name was Mr. MacIntyre. He later insisted I call him by his nickname, Mac.

Despite his limited background, Mac rose quickly through the ranks to serve as the plant's general foreman. He oversaw every area of the factory, and upon witnessing my allergic reaction, he knew I would never work in the tanyard. A young man incapable of working with the hides faced a worse fate. Thus began my labor as an office clerk.

As you mentioned in our meeting, important paperwork has a way of surfacing. That you are still watching for bubbles is baffling. Nevertheless, I too found advantage in paying attention to details, and since my job required stamping and filing, I saw every piece of paper that passed through the factory. From the beginning, Mac kept a close watch on my work. His manner left the impression he was taking me under his wing; however, he never counted on my intelligence. You see, Mr. Everett, I have been underestimated before.

I learned about payables, receivables, and supply orders. The more I learned, the more I grew interested in reading the documents I stamped. Mac explained any missing inventory as normal shortages and trivialized minor accounting discrepancies. This worked for a time. Still, my regard for Mac could not overshadow what I saw on a daily basis. At every opportunity, Mac ingratiated himself with Mr. Weston. Mr. Weston trusted Mac, but my father warned me about men who smile too wide. It turned out Mr. MacIntyre finagled himself into a position to embezzle thousands. Mr. Weston was crushed.

Do you see any similarities? A man with little experience elevated to a powerful position without justification. My blunder was not suspecting this sooner. I am distracted, but you, Mr. Everett, have little excuse. You must pursue this same line of reasoning. If Kennard has aligned himself with Mr. Harting for illicit purposes, he must be stopped before he can harm the Harting family. Embezzlers leave paper trails, Mr. Everett. One even a teenager found.

Sincerely,
Thomas M. Gadwell

March 28, 1889.

DEAR AVERY—

Sleep eludes me and with good reason. Last night there were strange noises in the stable. The previous night I know someone was skulking by the back door. Before you send for a doctor, months of living in my imagination is not playing tricks on me. I could show you the bruise from where I was held against a door. Never mind. You have no reason to believe one of my tales. To answer your question, yes, I am still working.

Thomas

March 31, 1889.

MY DARLING MARY—

I opened your letter with trembling hands then nearly tore it in half from delight. That you want me in your future no matter the reprisal from your family restores my faith in love. We will continue to pray for your father's blessing, but at last we can stroll in the sunshine among honorable folks. I am surprised we shall stroll together so soon.

Have I told you I am in love with a brilliant woman? Even if you had mentioned your family's acquaintance with Mrs. Winchester I never would have thought of it. I bow to your cunning. Your arrangement to spend a few months in Newport as Mrs. Winchester's companion has made my visit to Cousin Penelope look like the work of a novice. Am I right to fear you will use your wily ways on me? I think you already have.

Mary, you also alluded there is something you need to tell me. Does it have something to do with your father? I know this has been difficult. Once we are again together, maybe you will find it easier to tell me about Kansas and what happened. If it helps, you are not alone in your desire to air the rugs. Just last night, I at last learned why my father overlooks Fowler's many shortcomings.

Again confronted with a man slumped upon my doorstep pining the loss of an imaginary dog, I invited Fowler inside for strong coffee. Even through his slurred and meandering speech, I understood. Fowler was Father's paid substitute for the war. For eight hundred dollars and the promise of a job, Fowler fulfilled my father's military commitment. I do not know why that surprised me; I should be used to my father's lies by now.

How nerves have driven me to absurd tangents when you arrive in just a few days. I am uneasy with your arrival after dark and shall be at Mrs. Winchester's side when your steamer docks. My role as escort is not open for debate. Also, I should warn of Mrs. Winchester's growing quirks. Of late, she is often more than a bit eccentric. Just the other day she discharged the upstairs maid for not watering the silk topiaries. Still, overall I believe she is harmless.

My dearest, my delirium is proven. This letter will never reach you before you leave. Instead of mailing it I shall place it in your hands like a dimwit—an overjoyed dimwit.

Sealed with love,
Thomas

March 31, 1889.

AVERY—

For what purpose would you endure driving sleet and a temperamental artist? The new book is incomplete, and I prefer you wait until it is whole before tearing it apart. So when shall I expect you? I leave you to hire a carriage and navigate the unmarked streets on your own. Be warned I have no intention of playing host and am of the mind to kick you out without shame.

Must you really see me right away? Your timing is deplorable.

Thomas

March 31, 1889.

MR. EVERETT—

Your services are no longer required. Immediately cease all activity and post your final accounting. Regardless of our unfinished business, the continued risk and possibility that Mr. Kennard has discovered our dealings is too great a threat for me, and for those around me. It is imperative all records indicate our business has concluded. As your adherence to my wishes has thus far been unstable, I implore you to follow these demands. If not, someone could get hurt.

Thomas M. Gadwell

Spring 1889

April 10, 1889.

DEAR FATHER—

Weeks have disappeared into dazed memories I will someday confuse with dreams. I have been lost in my head and in my heart, but there is no excuse for leaving your emotional letter upon the kitchen table. I thought you impervious to the sourness of guilt, but as I read your list of regrets I embraced a man awakened by death. You deserve my reply.

Do you recall when I was seventeen and you asked what I would study at Harvard? How we had avoided the topic so long is a testament to our wills. As we sat in your study I thought my whole existence depended on that single dreaded answer. A bound copy of Poe's poems was in my lap, and I could hear Mother in the kitchen making bread. It was not our cook; Mother was pounding the dough to calm her nerves. I cleared my throat and proclaimed, "Law. My interest is in the law." Everyone proclaimed happiness for a year.

Mother's disappointment in my decision to change professions stung. On the other hand, I expected your contempt and considered it part of my artistic angst. My disregard for your opinion was as passionate as yours for mine. We were even, it seemed, until I brought home my first short story.

Mother read it in her sewing room. Her critique was guarded, but I believe she liked at least parts of it. To date, yours has been my most scathing review. Not only did you claim it painful to read, pubescent and trite, you said cavemen conveyed their message with more finesse.

As any son, I wanted your approval. So as your review of my work escalated into the apathy of my generation and the inevitable demise of the morality of our country, I decided I would never again seek your opinion. Though we have debated, argued, reasoned, and hassled, reflect for a moment and you will realize I have not sought your judgment on anything more consequential than need of a coat. I was satisfied with this arrangement until the postman delivered your letter of apology and explanation.

For years I agonized over why you hated my profession when it was you who encouraged me to love literature. That you were driven to give up your own aspirations is heartbreaking, and yet is it ever too late? You have admitted your jealousy, so it is now time to leave it in the past and start writing again. It would be an honor to read your work as a colleague.

As we speak of writing, have you ever wondered why I never asked your opinion of my first book? It was fear, but not that your critique would shame your earlier review. I was more afraid you never bothered to read it at all. Thank you for bothering. That you found it worthy of such high praise is my greatest achievement.

Since Pandora's Box is open, it seems a fitting time to ask for your guidance. By now Mother must have told you of my interest in a young lady. Mary is on the island acting as a companion to our neighbor, Mrs. Winchester. I have withheld this from Mother for fear she will swoop in to pick names for our unborn children. Though Mary has been here over a week, we are ill at ease and distracted. Granted, we have both been well occupied.

My writing remains involved and Mary runs endless errands for Mrs. Winchester. I have tried to catch Mary alone, but Mrs. Winchester thwarts my every move. Then when yesterday I was allowed a few minutes inside Winchester Manor, I left in relief. Once entranced by Mary's gentle singing, I found myself out of sorts as Mrs. Winchester encouraged Mary's incessant humming. I fled sporting a tremendous headache and foul mood. Love should eclipse such trivialities. Where are the harps and moonbeams?

In my short, but well-traveled, years I have learned we all seek ways to feel unique yet at the same time want solace in shared experiences. Did you ever encounter the same frustrations and worry? A difficult question for a new day, but I look no further than your love for Mother to know I ask the right man.

Father, we have all said and done that which we pray God will forgive before we can forgive ourselves. The world is grey, and sometimes the righteous linger in the shadows before seeking the light. I accept your apology and believe your remorse for your conspiracy with my friend, William Crawley. I have just a few unanswered questions I hope you concede need answering.

You said that when you ran into William in New York you found him distressed, that he readily confessed his unwitting part in the robbery at the Midland Bank in Worcester. Do you still believe his claim that he was not the counterfeiter? That, as a bank teller, he accidentally saw the phony bills? I find his willingness to accept a bribe to hide the plates instead of going to the police startling. Your involvement also leaves me dazed. His actions were both unscrupulous and illegal, and yet you put yourself in jeopardy to assist my old friend. Yes, indeed, the world is grey. My prayers are now for William's repentance.

Your loving son,
Thomas

April 19, 1889.

DEAR HENRY—

Your suggestion of a vicious dog is under advisement, despite your exploiting my distress to inspire a book title. A story called The Turn of the Screw? It sounds like a tradesman's manual. Then again, you might look dashing in shapeless trousers and a sporting cap.

By now you must have received my enthralling but brief letter announcing Mary's visit to Newport. I have kept a vigilant watch since her arrival, and at least for the time being it appears we are safe. The stress of it, however, is taking a toll. I wish I could convey things here were as chipper as the last stop on your European tour.

To my complete surprise and growing hostility, Mary insists we continue hiding our affections. We are caricatures of lovers drawn by a cheap novice and pretend a pleasant acquaintance in snapshots of placid outings. In fact, the ongoing concealment of our affair began the evening Mary arrived. A strong wind stirred the sea to angry waves, and the relentless rain so soaked the wooden dock it appeared to sag in the middle. It was a treacherous night on Newport Island—a forewarning had I paid attention.

I tried to remain calm as the minutes ticked by with the steamer nowhere in sight. But when Mary's ship was more than an hour late, I paced in front of an advertisement for salt by the pound and imagined the fiery sinking in such horrible detail I became light-headed and had to sit down. In my torment, I never considered the ramifications of such an outward display of concern while in the company of a woman who gossips for sport. It was a tell that revealed my hand to a more experienced, and fiendish, player.

At last the mooring lines were secured and Mary stood on the gangway. The tumultuous ride had ashened her cheeks and her gait was a bit unsteady, but she looked even more ravishing than I remembered. Upon seeing her for the first time in months I grinned like the useless joker card. In response she curtsied and said, "Mr. Gadwell, nice to see you again."

Once introductions were made, Mary turned her full attention to Mrs. Winchester and had little need for my assistance except for arranging transport of her trunks. I attempted polite conversation while longing to take her in my arms, but Mary was aloof and Mrs. Winchester had other plans.

Over the next few days my attempts to visit Mary were thwarted by Mrs. Winchester's butler who insisted the ladies were indisposed. At least with Mary tucked away I felt assured of her safety from island intruders and broken wheel clips. Thankfully, there are no new sightings of cigarette butts or reports from Mr. Everett. Then this morning a most implausible messenger delivered a special invitation.

"Thomas, you're looking well for an ill-tempered artist. I hope that rosy glow is from your writing and not some rare disease that requires two weeks at the spas in Baden Baden."

My agent stood at the door holding a travel case in one hand and an embossed envelope in the other.

"Avery? You made it after all. A bit disheveled and inconvenient, but here you are."

"I'm so fond of your quips, T. G., perhaps you should write a comedy." Avery handed me the envelope, stepped over the threshold, and put down his satchel. With a flourish, he took off his raincoat and posed with his hands on his hips.

We chuckled in short bursts that swelled when Avery

spun in a circle. I stared at a middle-aged man in round wire glasses wearing a lime-green dinner jacket with purple buttons. When I told him he was a rare vision, he opened his satchel and retrieved a matching hat.

"You found a green Bollinger? I don't believe it," I said.

"I brought it for you, T. G. I have exciting news."

I know his stylish ensemble makes little sense to you, Henry, but Avery and I have always enjoyed a bit of tomfoolery.

As Avery's updates are sweeter than Swiss bell ringers, I first suggested he warm himself by the fire. I have learned to steel myself for Avery's good news, which is a combination of conjecture and wishful thinking.

We exchanged pleasantries that included the inspirational successes of another client (I was inspired to light a Cuban) and the passionate details of Avery's latest invention.

"So, wait, you're telling me there are metal teeth that overlap and hold fabric together tighter than a button? Whose teeth?" I asked.

"Not real teeth for heaven's sake. Who in the world would give me their teeth? It's made from metal coils that remind me of teeth, and so, well, you understand. I've only begun the drawings but it could be revolutionary, truly revolutionary. I'm working on a coat that won't gap and shoes without laces, and—"

"Not on finding another publisher for *The Awakening of Foster Green.*"

He claimed peddling my second book for months without sleep. I countered his lack of sleep was from convincing pretty girls at the groggery he had forgotten his specs and needed them to read him the wine list.

"Touché, but if that were true I couldn't report we have

a bite on the line. That's why I'm here with your hat, Thomas. I sent *Foster Green* to Putnam. To my unequaled delight, short of tinkering in my shed on Saturday afternoons, they're interested in a two-book contract."

I recalled similar enthusiasm with Harpers, so I implored Avery to understand if I refrained from joyous dancing and donning that preposterous hat. Avery seemed disappointed in my guarded attitude but bounced back by handing me Putnam's notes for *Foster* and demanding I complete the simple edits before continuing with my new book. "Or do you first have to build a doghouse for your pet emu?" he asked.

I agreed to his agenda in exchange for feedback on the new story. Avery took off the jacket and went straight to work. With Avery locked away in my study, I spent the rest of this afternoon excited about his special delivery.

The invitation is for dinner this evening. In fact, I have an idea and must leave you here to get ready. I may just have thought of a way to at last capture a few moments alone with Mary.

With veneration,
Thomas

April 19, 1889.

DEAR ABIGAIL—

Thank you for the invitation to join you for dinner. I accept with gratitude and ask for a small indulgence in allowing me to bring an unexpected houseguest. He is a fine gent, and I trust you will enjoy his fetish.

Until this evening,

Thomas

April 25, 1889.

DEAR HENRY—

Your telegram was so enthusiastic, you forgot to mention when you sail for home. How fortunate to find a porthole in history. I have read about the RMS Etruria in the news. Do you think the captain can break the record? Crossing the Atlantic in less than a week makes me think of a dog with his tail on fire. Stay away from the stern. It will likely pitch from the speed.

When last I wrote, Avery and I were headed to Abigail's for dinner. Though our argument lasted until we had to leave, Avery agreed to accompany me in the hideous green coat and hat in exchange for additional draft pages locked in my desk drawer. I thought the whimsy might distract Abigail. Had the dinner gone as planned, I would leave you to here to imagine napkin rings and salmon croquettes. The evening turned into a spectacle, but not because of Avery's stylish jacket.

We found Abigail waiting for us in the parlor. I introduced Avery and was humored when she sneered and asked if his work as a literary agent required such "bizarre attire." As Avery's nostrils flared, I interjected how well Abigail looked. She wore a formal teal gown. It was one of the few times I had seen her without an animal mask or powdered wig.

"Thank you, dear. I do prefer costume parties and anything with feathers, I'm sure *you* understand Mr. Avery, but I didn't think it appropriate tonight. Not when I'm sharing my house with a young lady obviously without such fancies," she said.

I asked how she and her companion were getting along.

"A lovely girl with exceptional manners, well-trained I believe, although," she paused, "I find her chatter a bit, shall we say, tiresome. I'm sure it's just nerves or the sea air. It has such a raw bite this time of year she may be moving her mouth just to keep warm."

Avery chuckled. If not for Mrs. Winchester's immobile gaze, I would have elbowed him in the side. Then movement on the staircase caused us all to turn.

"There you are, Mary," Mrs. Winchester said. "Well, my dress looks stunning on you. Don't you agree, Thomas? What a marvelous figure you have my dear. I can hardly remember myself so petite, but then in some areas I was more, shall we say, endowed. Oh how youth escapes so quickly. Come, come, the other guests shall be here and I've changed my mind and want to entertain in the living room this evening."

Before I could make introductions, Avery chuckled at Mary and trotted after Mrs. Winchester. I, however, could not look away.

Mary's dress had faded to a dull orange that hinted it may have once been scarlet. Trimmed in yellowed lace, a tall velvet collar sagged against Mary's face. Her delicate shoulders were lost in fabric and the dropped waistline skirt, out of fashion even in my mother's prime, was so long Mary was holding up the skirt to keep it from dragging on the floor.

I commented the dress looked lovely, to which she said, "Funny, Thomas. You're very funny. She insisted I wear this dreadful thing." She turned toward the door and stepped closer to me. She was close enough to embrace as she explained Abigail refused to come down to dinner unless she put on the gown. "She acted like a three-year-old," she whispered. "Thomas, you failed to mention in your letters that she's plumb crazy. She'd make a marvelous character for your next book, my love."

I think she mentioned something about keeping notes but I heard little beyond Mary calling me her love.

Mary then asked about my company. "He has gall looking at me like I'm off my nut."

I explained the galling lad was my agent and the garb my doing. It seemed my whim might help the evening's situation. Mary wanted to know what he was doing in Newport, but that was still unanswered.

"Never mind him. Are you well? I couldn't have waited another minute to see you. She must have you frantic."

"You could call it that. There's really too much to tell you before dinner, but I'm going to the market tomorrow. I'll be there at noontime when the eggs are fresh and the store well-stocked. She must have said it had to be noon at least four times. If I return with eggs that have even the tiniest spot she'll be upset, and no, her girl can't go because she's washing sheets and simply won't have time." Mary fluttered her hands and shook her head. "Anyway, I'm sure you must need something from the market now that you have a houseguest."

Mrs. Winchester called for me to come see her new crab spider. I leaned close and pressed my lips to Mary's ear. I felt her warm breath shudder on my neck. "I've missed you," I whispered.

"Mary!" Mrs. Winchester shrieked.

Mary jumped, knocking me in the jaw. She apologized then grabbed a wad of the long skirt. "Thomas, please tell her I'll be right in. I have to pin this or I'm afraid I'll tumble over it."

The other guests arrived as I joined Mrs. Winchester and Avery in the living room so I was spared another viewing of spiders pinned to cardboard. Introductions were made to the Duniways from Connecticut, a stately couple on the island to handle a household crisis.

Seems Abigail saw their house girl wearing the mistress's chinchilla coat around town. Mrs. Duniway was beside herself with gratitude for Abigail's letter. On the other hand, Mr. Duniway wanted to know why in the world his wife needed a fur coat in summer. The building tiff was interrupted by movement at the door. We turned. Mary stood in the doorway.

She had indeed attempted to pin the dress, and it was a valiant effort but of little use. If not for her twisted hair secured by a pearl clip and the composed, delicate way she carried her slight frame, I would have mistaken her for a gutterpup.

Mrs. Winchester waved her arms in a grand sweeping motion as she presented her companion, Miss Harting from New York. I then expected her to explain the dress, perhaps share that it was sentimental and she had asked Mary to wear it as a reminder of a departed relative. Mrs. Winchester remained silent as her guests gaped.

Mr. Duniway looked at Avery. "I can dismiss you as one of those creative sorts who wants attention," he said, then turned to Mary, "but what is this?"

Mary picked up her skirt, rustled it side to side, and grinned. "I'm told it's the latest fashion from Paris," she said.

Mrs. Winchester huffed. "I hope you didn't think Newport too artless to appreciate fashion. Your joke is not at all amusing, Miss Harting."

Mary was stunned—but just for a second. She bowed with ease and asked we accept her apologies while she changed into something more appropriate. Mrs. Winchester stopped her, claiming there was not enough time before dinner and she did not want the food to get cold. This was when Avery turned to me and said, "Wait, the girl in San Diego?" This time I did elbow him in the side. Avery got the message to hold his tongue, but Mrs. Winchester saw our exchange and frowned.

"Harting from New York? Is your father Charlton Harting?" Mr. Duniway asked.

Mary's voice caught when she asked if he knew her father.

"Only of him," he said, then turned from Mary and demanded a tall gin.

Cocktails were served and small talk included the long winter blamed for souring the stock market, Avery's complaint of bootleg printing in Europe, and Abigail's obscure reference to a Vaudevillian act none of us had seen. Mary was polite, but quiet, and I was distracted by Mrs. Winchester's malicious game. At last dinner was served; however, the addition of silverware only provided an excuse for the stilted conversation.

Mary asked Mrs. Duniway when they would return to Newport. Mrs. Duniway asked her husband who replied, "In the summer." Mrs. Duniway turned to Mary and said, "In the summer."

In a gallant effort, Mary then turned to Mr. Duniway and asked how he knew of her father. He waved his knife at her. "That's not dinner conversation," he said. Mrs. Winchester barked for the servers to clear the plates and bring the lamb at once.

We continued in silence, though Mr. Duniway had a raucous way of chewing, and our misery at last ended when Mrs. Duniway announced a headache just as dessert was cleared. I was buttoning my coat by the front door when Mrs. Winchester tapped me on the shoulder and asked me to stay. There was something she wanted to discuss with me. I looked to Avery.

"Oh, your houseguest can go with Clara and Walter," Mrs. Winchester said. Neither looked enthusiastic but agreed.

I watched the carriage pull away then turned to confront Abigail. There was something I wanted to discuss with her too.

"She went back into the parlor," Mary said.

Mary and I were alone. I stepped toward her, straightening my tie and flashing a wide smirk, but Mrs. Winchester bellowed and Mary did not want to keep her waiting.

Mrs. Winchester stood by the fading fire with her arms wrapped around her like a child in the snow. As I stepped forward, Abigail sighed. "Oh, my dear, Mary, I'm so sorry. I say and do things even I don't understand. My doctors have no idea why, only that it may have something to do with my brain. It could be a hemorrhage or even a tumor. I think it must be a tumor. I can feel it growing. Oh, I just know it'll get so big I won't be able to pick up my head."

Mary glanced at me but all I could do was shrug.

Mary led Mrs. Winchester to the flowered settee then rang the servant's bell and asked for three strong cups of tea.

"Make it two," Mrs. Winchester added. "Thomas, you must go. I want to speak with Mary alone. Thank you for coming. I'll see you soon."

It was so abrupt and unsettling that I left Mary sitting on the loveseat patting Mrs. Winchester's hand, her expression that of tender compassion mixed with confusion.

Though the awful dinner is over, the folly continues. Can I share the subsequent decline? It is maddening.

The following afternoon I left Avery in the library with my revisions and went to the market to meet Mary. I wanted to know if Mrs. Winchester had explained herself. I loitered in front of the market for an hour, but Mary never showed up. Overcome by visions of henchmen in bushes, I went straight to Winchester Manor.

From the doorstep the butler assured me Mary was inside and had not left all day. I begged entry, but the madam was not up to accepting visitors. The butler closed the door without further explanation.

As soon as I returned home I wrote a note inviting Mrs. Winchester and her temporary companion for tea the next afternoon. I dispatched Mr. Fowler and was tickled by a quick reply. Mrs. Winchester was too fatigued for tea, but Mary was free to go unless she was needed. My delight was short lived.

The next day I endured one of the worst of my literary career. Putnam's "simple edits" for *Foster* included reworking the entire second half, and Avery described my new story as unimaginative and without a clear audience. I tried to explain, but Avery compared my drafts with other writers in his care and emphasized his deep concern no less than five times.

Nearing two o'clock, the appointed time for tea, I handed Avery his hat and directed him to Mrs. Potter's for fish fry and cobbler.

"Is someone calling? Mary, perhaps? She's extremely handsome; however, the last thing you need right now is a damsel in distress. At least now I understand the trip to New York. I should have known."

"Have a nice afternoon, Avery. Don't get lost on your way back."

Ten minutes later, I heard a soft knock on the door. I was so excited I tripped on the braided hall rug and caught myself on the door handle. I thrust opened the door with boyish delight to discover a lad in a thick Cavalry coat holding out an envelope. Mrs. Winchester apologized for Mary's absence and declared Mary a dear to stay and help an old woman who felt like "the underside of a barge."

Since then, I have hand-delivered flyers about upcoming town elections and asked to borrow coffee, but Abigail will not let me in or Mary out. As I write these words, Henry, my blood is hot. I must do something—anything.

Thomas

April 29, 1889.

DEAR MOTHER—

Thank you for the brown bread and cherry preserves. Your package came as a nice surprise, and I was thoroughly buttered up by the time I read the enclosed note. Father held out longer than I expected. How did you persuade him to tell you? Yes, Mary is still in Newport but you need not worry. Our scarce time together is not worthy of summertime gossip. Plus, my agent, Avery, arrived just in time to catalogue my writing flaws and play chaperone.

Do you remember Avery from the Easter party? He was the man Father seized by the arm to badger about paper manufacturing. After an hour, the poor man looked ready to gnaw off his own arm. Avery left yesterday morning. Before catching the ferry, however, he cornered me in the kitchen. His grim expression was halting. Then when he began scratching his head, I prepared for the worst. Avery's itchy scalp means bad news.

To his credit, Avery managed to convince Putnam to buy two books. Before you plan a celebratory dinner, there is a caveat. I must have final edits of my second book and a polished draft of a third finished by the middle of June. It was the first I had heard of a deadline. The panic on my face prompted Avery to offer me one of the padded dining room chairs.

The time constraint is my own fault. The publishing world is small, and Harpers gave an unflattering reference about my punctuality. I recall similar remarks about turning in homework assignments on time. Even so, Putnam is giving me a second chance. But if I miss the deadline (in which case Avery will kill me), they pull the deal. As Avery puts it, "You either submit the work on time or they cross you off and go on to the next author. It's that simple for them."

Mother, this seems a daunting task. How can I write well under duress? Avery is convinced I can meet the deadline if I rid myself of distractions. He, of course, means Mary.

When Avery stopped me, I was on my way to find Mary. My determination to see Mary matches Mrs. Winchester's resolve to keep her from me. At least in this instance, my tenacity was rewarded. Mary and I managed to slip away for a few hours. As you delight in a bit of romance, I feel obliged to share this with you.

The brisk morning air held a dense mist that settled like a stout man awaiting his dinner. I considered taking the carriage but feared drawing attention to visiting Mary without a plausible excuse. As I considered my options, I remembered Mrs. Winchester's ridicule of Mary's pedestrian habits. Walking was not only foolhardy but leads to all manner of illnesses, not the least of which is flat feet. Mrs. Winchester scolded Mary for her daily sojourns—at least three turns through the gardens and one pass around the front drive. I thus decided to walk.

What felt quick in a carriage, grew quite tiresome on foot. By the time I reached the Winchester's drive, mud weighed my boots and my face was damp from mist and sweat. I unwrapped a turn of my wool scarf and searched for Mary. It was a senseless desire, but I hoped against reason I would arrive just as Mary was coming out for her walk. The driveway was empty.

I waited by the street for a few minutes, feeling rather conspicuous and more than a bit like a bluenose. To avoid the police captain and anyone having a reason to flag you down at the Independence Day parade, I strolled down the drive until I found an opening behind the hedges. Since I saw no one watching, I pressed myself behind the bushes, tearing a small hole in my overcoat and scraping my knuckles on the thorny overgrowth. If you are now worried your son is a lout, I submit even a gentleman must sometimes take extraordinary measures.

Waiting in the frigid, wet wind did nothing to improve my mood. Even the thought of seeing Mary could not overshadow the dread of a new deadline. My legs stiffened and lips burned, and after hopping in place and breathing into cupped hands I considered Mary might fear the looming clouds and choose a book and stoked fire. I began chastising myself for a brainless idea that wasted precious time, when I heard footsteps on the gravel drive. I called out Mary's name. She jumped.

Instead of a bright smile, she tightened the black wrap around her chin and wanted to know what in the world I was doing. My explanation prompted Mary to shake her head and ask, "And it never occurred to you to knock on the front door?"

Even if it had, I doubted getting past the butler. I tried to explain but Mary held my gaze and said in a soft voice, "I wish you had come sooner. You have no idea what's been going on in that house."

Though I encouraged her to tell me what was wrong, Mary's description of Mrs. Winchester's antics confirmed a growing suspicion about our new neighbor. You must come to Newport prepared.

Mary moved about as if admiring the bushes while she explained. "It's not just one thing, it's everything. At first I thought Mrs. Winchester was just quirky and a little unorganized, but I think I was too kind. Truly, I believe she's as nutty as a fruitcake. Did you know she changes her plans all day long? One moment she'd like breakfast then the next just milk and a carriage ride to the bluffs. Once the horses are bridled, it's too cold and she's decided to stay in and read. She pulls books from the library, scans the front and back cover, sighs and tosses them aside—"

I interrupted, claiming I sometimes found myself unsure of what I wanted to read.

"Sometimes, yes, but she does it for hours while I must sit and watch. Then she wants to read aloud, of course once she can find the right book. I usually enjoy listening to someone read, but she skips sentences and mispronounces words seemingly on purpose. Then she laughs and says the mistake is of no consequence to the story." Mary ran her gloved hand across her forehead. "Is it possible for someone to drive you crackers?"

"This isn't working. I feel ridiculous talking through weeds," I said.

"Now you feel ridiculous?" she replied.

I ignored her retort and parted the bushes. Mary squeezed through and I took her hand. Not wanting Mary to suffer on my account, I suggested it might be well advised for her to go back home. Perhaps my wording was clumsy, but I meant the sentiment as a comfort. Mary's eyes welled with tears.

"Thomas, don't you want to spend time with me? I'm upset and irritated, but I still want to see you. You've been so tense since I got here. Is that because you want me to leave?"

When I told her how much I wanted her to stay, she fell against my chest and I hugged her. I kissed the top of her head and smoothed her wind-cast hair.

"I'm being so fragile, and my nerves are a jumble. I just can't relax. She's always watching me and listening at corners. I can't even write you a note for fear she'll read it. I just know she will. This is just so infuriating. I've thought of almost nothing else but seeing you again. Instead I'm imprisoned with those disgusting bugs."

When you meet Mrs. Winchester this summer, you must claim to have a lethal allergy to all kinds of bugs, specifically spiders. Trust me on this.

Mary broke our embrace and let out a long breath. She looked at me with damp eyes as she pulled a leaf from my hair.

"So you admit imagining us together?" I said.

Her shy grin raised both our spirits. Warmth radiated from her smile, wisps of hair swirled around her cheeks, and her hand was still in mine. Without forethought, I pulled her toward me and kissed her. She kissed me for a moment then pulled away. Her blush deepened as she looked at the ground with the embarrassment of a schoolgirl.

"Thomas, this isn't proper."

I placed my index finger under her chin and raised her head. She was beaming. I kissed her again. This time she leaned close and wrapped her arms around my neck. Captured by joy, I never heard the carriage.

Mary jerked away just as a coach passed. "Mrs. Winchester will hear of lovers frozen in a secret embrace. That would definitely ruin her day," Mary said.

A glorious way to end, I say.

With Mary out of reach and shuffling from the wind, I suggested it was too cold to stay outside. Mrs. Winchester, however, required canned peaches and Mary was on her way to the market. She asked if I would escort her into town and give her a tour. Even after three weeks, she had seen little of our winter haven. I could think of nothing finer.

"Wait here and I'll get the carriage," she said. "It's definitely too brisk to walk."

"I know a way to warm you up."

"That, sir, is why I'm fetching the carriage."

The next two hours were bliss. We rode to the market nestled beside each other and reminisced about New York and California. When the road was empty we held hands, and just before we turned onto Bellevue Avenue, she kissed my cheek and pressed her cold nose against my neck.

After the market, I led the carriage past the charming cottages and shops on Ocean Drive. Then we rode along the shore by Fort Adams before I stopped the carriage on the west bluff. Thick clouds skirted across the sky. Mary burrowed closer.

"The climate of the sea," I said, then slipped my arm around her shoulder. "Did you enjoy the climate in Abilene?"

Mary stiffened at the mention, saying there was nothing she enjoyed about Abilene. I gathered that much from her letters, or really lack of letters. I squeezed her shoulders and asked if she wanted to tell me more.

She gazed at me for a moment then turned away. "I will, Thomas. I want to, I really do, but not right now. I don't feel like talking about that right now. This has been such a pleasant afternoon. Let's not ruin it."

My curiosity heightened, but I nodded and changed the subject to how her sister was feeling. Mary's tone darkened as she launched into her sister's difficult pregnancy. The doctors insist she must lie-in for the next few weeks until the baby is due. Mary is not only concerned for her sister's health; she feels guilty for wanting to leave Newport to see the newborn.

A loud crack of thunder startled us both and a strong breeze shook the carriage.

"I'd better get you back," I said. "That's Newport's promise of an angry storm."

We chatted about Newport on the ride back, but my thoughts were on figuring out a way to see her again. Then when I steered the horses down Mrs. Winchester's drive, Mary gasped. Mrs. Winchester stood in the doorway with her hands on her hips.

"I suppose stopping the carriage to coax you into a proper goodbye is out of the question," I said.

Mary smiled behind her hand. "Did you have something in mind?"

"Most definitely."

When we reached the house, Mrs. Winchester flung aside the door as one casts off bedcovers and marched toward the carriage. I helped Mary to the ground and stood beside her.

"I suppose you enjoy frightening an old woman to her grave, young lady." Mrs. Winchester scowled at me and added, "I see what's kept you so long. I nearly sent out a search party. I was at my wits' end with worry that you were blown into the sea. Really, Miss Harting, you should show more courtesy. You're a guest in my home and I will not tolerate insubordination."

Mary nodded, but I stepped in front of her and bowed. "It's I who must apologize, Abigail. Mary insisted we hurry back, but I've been so confined and consumed with my writing, and Miss Harting was kind enough to indulge me. I had no idea the hour was this late. Please accept my apologies."

Mrs. Winchester shook her head. "Go home, Thomas. I

won't spend all evening worrying about you too. Go quickly before the storm hits." Mrs. Winchester huffed, then pivoted like a Union soldier and disappeared into the house.

Mary allowed me to walk her up the steps but did not offer her hand.

"Thank you, Mr. Gadwell. I hope we see you again soon," she said. Mary curtsied then leaned toward me. "But no bushes," she whispered.

The storm was indeed fierce. For several days I confined myself to the study. Though you may find this hard to understand, it was marvelous. Creative ideas burst forth like tulips through the bitter earth, and I wrote with a zeal I thought lost.

The storm is over, but I am unable to stop working. Mary and her soft kisses haunt me, yet I feel desperate to finish on time. I must pull myself away. A full week has passed with clear skies. What will Mary think? Perhaps I understand a little better why Henry prefers bachelorhood. My approaching deadline is pressing. But so is my guilt.

Your loving son,
Thomas

May 6, 1889.

HELLO, AVERY—

I found the note you left in the pantry. The accompanying box of pen nibs was a nice touch.

No need to worry, good chap, I sniffed out my lucky socks. The fifteenth of June or else—I shall scratch the date in my forearm.

T. G.

May 7, 1889.

DEAR HENRY—

If you were here slouched on the chaise washing down my melancholy with Irish coffee, you would tell me to sift through my torment for book fodder. I shall endure your firm hand if you allow a man must first purge his thoughts to see them clearly. My affair is like a tragic fable. I just wish I could blame Mary's trickery and lies on a magic potion. Pray my seeping wounds dry with the ink.

I arrived at Winchester Manor just in time for afternoon tea. It was a presumptive gesture, but I needed to apologize to Mary for disappearing. For the first time, Henry, my writing imprisoned me in an overwhelming, maddening anxiety to perfect each word. You are correct; passion is not for the frail. But those outside the wondrous experience see only the neglect it causes. To my surprise, the butler let me in without an argument and directed me to the front sitting room where Mrs. Winchester was cataloging specimens. A fight, however, was still to come.

Mrs. Winchester raised her head from thick piles of cardboard and jars of milky liquid. She wore a full black dress with a high lace collar and swung a pair of magnifying spectacles between her thumb and index finger. "What brings you here today, Thomas? Mary, I suppose." I found her biting tone filled with detestable innuendo most inappropriate.

She listened with a bland expression as I asked forgiveness for my rude behavior in staying away so long. I believed her shrug meant to show indifference, but then she suggested I stay for tea. She tossed her glasses onto the cluttered workbench and led me to the drawing room.

I commented on the nice sunshine after the terrible storm and asked how her window fared. The window in

Mary's room leaked but Abigail felt repairs could wait until summer. I offered to send Fowler right over, but Abigail was incensed. "I'll not hear another word, Thomas. I'm perfectly capable of taking care of my own affairs." As I followed Abigail into the parlor, I worried for Mary's physical health as well as her mental state.

Mary entered wearing a plain cream colored gown beneath a thick brown shawl. Her cheeks were pale and her lips drawn as she sat opposite Mrs. Winchester and filled our teacups before her own. "Mr. Gadwell, to what do we owe the pleasure?"

I cleared my throat. "As I was just explaining, I'm here to apologize for my abrupt absence. I would have been here sooner if not for the weather and, well, getting carried away with my work. I've neglected you both and am ashamed of myself."

Mrs. Winchester inquired how my word-smithing was going, to which I gave a quick outline. "But enough of that. You don't want to get me started or I might ramble all afternoon."

"Don't be so modest, Mr. Gadwell," Mary said. "Hearing of your little novel is rather intriguing. In fact it sounds so simple, really. I should think anyone could give it a try."

Mrs. Winchester's face lit up. She clapped and chimed in how she finds reading easy enough. She wanted to know if writing was so simple.

"That's a matter of opinion I assure you. Nevertheless, I do sincerely apologize again for my delay."

Mary waved her hand as if dismissing a servant and said there was no need. My hackles rose.

We sat in uncomfortable silence while Mrs. Winchester added three sugar cubes and a healthy pour of cream to her tea. Then all of sudden Mrs. Winchester began gushing about Miss Petrova and how she was taking lessons in Cambridge, right near my family home, and was receiving high praise. She pulled a clipping from her pocket and shoved it in my hand.

"Isn't that a lovely rendering? And what a talent. The dear girl writes only that she's enjoying herself tremendously. She's so modest." She turned to Mary. "She really is a beauty, isn't that so, Thomas?"

When I made no reply, Mrs. Winchester continued. According to Mrs. Winchester, I had somehow made an impression on Miss Petrova. Why else, she concluded, would the young lady ask Mrs. Winchester to send her regards. My only reply was to ask Mrs. Winchester if she read Russian.

"Russian, oh dear me, no. She's been taking English lessons at a fantastic pace. Beauty and intelligence is such a rare combination, don't you think? Well, I must finish my needlepoint for the charity auction. I'm sure, Thomas, you prefer chatting with a pretty young girl than an old crane like me." She eyed Mary. "Men are so fickle, don't you agree, Mary? I'll be in the sewing room, within earshot I remind you. Thomas, you mind your manners. I don't believe the gossip I hear about you, but, still, a young woman must take precautions. Ta ta." She plucked the clipping from my hold before sweeping from the room with unexpected nimbleness.

I began to question what in the world she was talking about, when Mary shook her head and asked in a loud voice about the weather on the ride over. Mary nodded toward the door and pointed to her ears. I heard the floorboards creak on the other side of the door followed by muffled footsteps leading down the hall.

"Now she's gone. She likes to eavesdrop."

"I gather. What was that nonsense about my being fickle and town gossip?"

"Oh, you haven't heard? You're madly in love with Miss Katya Petrova, the extremely beautiful and talented opera singer. The fortune teller from Thanksgiving even predicted it. Mrs. Winchester has spoken of nothing else for the past week; ever since she got a letter from the Russian goddess.

"You two are the perfect couple," Mary continued. "She's tall, much taller than me, a perfect height for you. She has long dark hair, longer than mine, thicker too, with lovely amber highlights. Isn't it a shame I don't have highlights like Miss Petrova."

"What are you talking about? What's wrong with that woman?"

Mary put down her teacup and moved to the fireplace. She faced me with her back pressed against the marble mantle and asked if I did anything to encourage the opera singer. From Mrs. Winchester's account, I was a tongue-tied schoolboy who practically drooled the night we first met. Mary mentioned my infatuation with talented musicians, but I stopped her.

"If you're speaking of Rebecca," I paused, "I mean, Gertrude, this is quite a different situation. And I didn't drool. I hardly paid her any attention at Thanksgiving. She didn't even speak English." I stood up and faced Mary. "This is ludicrous. I have no interest in Miss Petrova. I was polite, she was polite, but that was all. She's pretty, I suppose, but not in any way I found remarkable or even that memorable. That night, every night, I think of you. You're so much more beautiful, Mary. You mustn't believe Abigail's idle chatter."

Mary sighed. "I don't. I believe you, Thomas. Really, I

do. I'm at my wit's end. It's that ill-tempered woman and her—"

I suggested she ignore Abigail, but Mary gave a bitter laugh and claimed ignoring her was impossible. After hearing the routine Mary had shouldered for five weeks, I had to agree.

While I burrow in my study, Mrs. Winchester wakes Mary in the middle of the night to share gossip from the maids. Over breakfast she rambles until Mary's ears ring. By lunch Mrs. Winchester has read to Mary for at least two hours (an inconceivable chore by anyone's standards), and then Mary is dragged into the foundry to help identify bugs. By nightfall Mary is exhausted, yet evening cake is served with tears about a brain tumor and Mrs. Winchester's impending death.

"Why didn't you warn me?" Mary asked.

I had no idea she was so grueling and shared this with Mary. My mistake was adding that Mrs. Winchester never acted so strangely with me.

"Are you implying this is somehow my fault?"

"Of course not." I sat back down and motioned for her to do the same. She shook her head and remained standing. "Mary, you mustn't stay here. You're obviously exhausted, and she's completely incorrigible. You should go home and rest. See your sister. I'll meet you soon." She mistook my intent.

"I look exhausted? Oh, never mind that. I can't leave when it's obvious she wants me to. Don't you see, Thomas, she's playing games. It all began with that horrible dress."

I had almost forgotten about the medieval frock and asked if Abigail explained her antics. Mary told me that as soon as I left that night, Abigail's tears dried up and she went straight off to bed. Nothing had been said about it since.

"I don't understand why, but I think this has something to do with you," Mary said. "She's attached to you in some way."

As Mary left the fireplace to take a turn around the room, she speculated about a tragic dead son or whether I might represent the son Abigail always wanted. I watched Mary's brow twitch as she paced with her hands clasped behind her back. Held by her concentration, for the first time I looked at Mary without her becoming self conscious and turning away. Worry struck me like Malcolm's fist in the fourth grade. She was rare and precious; far too precious to lose.

"Mary, please sit down. A man can only watch a handsome creature strut about for so long. Keep pacing and I'm afraid I'll lose my status as a gentleman."

She stopped, and a faint blush rose from her chest. "You always know just what to say. Someone taught you well."

I wanted to know what she meant and asked if she thought of me as some sort of Casanova. She made a good point.

"Shouldn't I wonder about a man who spends hours writing dialogue?"

I felt edgy from the obvious strain between us, but instead of a quip I told her I was not well versed in womanly innuendo and asked that she tell me plainly what she was driving at.

"I suppose that's fair because I don't understand you sometimes, either. You want it plain? All right then. You've got a well-polished silver tongue which I first noticed at the hotel. Maybe the moonlight softened the edges but don't think I haven't questioned your skills. If I didn't know you and happened to overhear you enticing another young lady, I might think you some sort of smooth talking bilker."

I imagined a man with thick side whiskers pitching hair cream from a cart and chuckled. "A bilker? Me?"

Mary tipped her chin to hide a smile.

"What gave me away?" I asked, "Was it my finely choreographed stumbling or maybe the stuttering at your father's dinner table?"

We laughed together for the first time in months, though exhaustion and tension fueled our jittery amusement. While I caught my breath, I asked if she really found me puzzling when most of the time I felt like a bumbling gull.

"All men are a bit of a mystery to our sex. Look at my father and his antics. He actually calls you . . ." she paused with wide eyes. "Do you want to know?"

I assured her not much was worse than what I had long imagined.

She took a breath. "He says you're just another gadabout wasting your father's money and using fancy words to—"

"I get it."

"I'm sorry. I just can't say anything to change his mind." She stepped forward and collapsed into a burgundy wing-back chair across from the couch. "When I was in Abilene, I tried to tell him how I feel about you, but he wouldn't listen. He told me I'm too young to know what's important. Did you know you're just a silly girl's infatuation? He actually said a new gable hat with a pretty lace veil would cure me. What could I say to something so stupid?"

She went on to tell me how they fought constantly. When they were alone, he accused her of being ungrateful. Then when others were around, he fawned over her. Mary was shocked and revolted by his behavior, and by the time she left Abilene they were barely speaking to each other.

Mary looked frail and despondent. I wanted to take her hand, tell her everything would be fine, but the sense of worry had returned.

She wrung her hands together before running them over the folds in her skirt. "When I was a girl, Father would take me for cake after church. Just me, while Sarah practiced her piano. He'd order two large slices of chocolate and let me talk about anything. He asked about school and my friends and listened as if there were nothing more important. I was his princess.

"In Abilene he ordered me to stop acting like a selfish child and hollered for my silence before I could even finish a sentence. I don't know what I've done to make him so angry, but he looks at me as if he has no use for me. I think he hates me." She paused to wipe her eyes with the back of her hand. "He's broken my heart, Thomas."

I was about to take Mary into my arms when the parlor door flung open. Mrs. Winchester stood at the threshold holding knitting needles and a ball of blue yarn. Mary turned away, but not fast enough.

"Thomas, what have you done? I feel more like knitting so I came to ask what color scarf you'd like and I find my young companion's face all flushed and puffy."

Mary assured Mrs. Winchester I had done nothing and her tears were over all the immigrant children in New York dying from rheumatic fever.

"Oh . . . yes . . . that, well . . . tragic." Mrs. Winchester opened her mouth, closed it, and then looked at me. "Blue it is, and Thomas, please help Miss Harting find more uplifting topics to discuss. It's all very depressing and unladylike."

Mrs. Winchester turned to leave then stopped. "I almost

forgot. I have another letter for you, Mary, from your admirer." She waved a thick tan envelope with a bright red seal. "You may have competition, dear Thomas. But then how could any girl resist your gentle smile and thoughtful brown eyes—unless of course she's sensible enough to consider your irregular occupation." She shrugged. "Well, here you are, Mary, dear."

She placed the letter on the table closest to me then left. My jaw tightened. Mary stood up, went to the table, and examined the seal.

Henry, a knock at the door. Mary has come to apologize!

Thomas

May 9, 1889.

DEAR HENRY—

A day has passed, though, after my indulgence at the pub, much of yesterday is still missing. The person at my door, you see, was not Mary.

I believe I left off with Mrs. Winchester barging into the parlor with a letter for Mary. Did I yet say who it was from? The letter was from Lowell Kennard. Upon hearing his name, the rising tension pressed in against me. The cool room turned suddenly stuffy and uncomfortable. If only I had paused to open the window or take a deep breath for sake of tone. I did not pause—nor did Mary.

My first question was why the Muskrat was writing to her in Newport—why he was writing to her at all.

"Please don't call him a muskrat," she said. "I should never have used that name. It's very cruel."

My chest tightened. "Of course. I wouldn't want to offend the fine gent. I take it you're in contact with Mr. Kennard?"

With her face drawn and eyes fixed on the Persian rug, she told me he was in contact with her. She suspected her mother gave him her address. I remained calm and in a flat voice suggested she open the letter. But when Mary just shook her head and mumbled it was likely nothing, my tranquil façade cracked.

"If it's nothing, then why are your hands trembling? I demand to know what's in that letter, Mary. I think I have a right to know."

She looked at me for a moment, appearing ready to argue, but then nodded in agreement. Her admission that she "should have told me sooner" did nothing to soothe the growing knot in my stomach.

Mary opened the envelope and circled the room as she

skimmed the letter. She folded it in half, pushed it deep into the pocket of her dress, and stopped behind the wing-back chair. I would later reflect she held the chair as a shield.

"You'll have to forgive my bluntness, but I don't think I can say this any other way." She squeezed the chair and sighed. "The night before I left Abilene, Lowell Kennard asked me to marry him."

Marry him? She had seen Kennard? Where? When?

"I know you don't understand, Thomas. That's my fault." She lowered her eyes. "I didn't tell you because it didn't matter. But now he wants my answer."

Her expression was filled with despair. She felt sorry for the Muskrat. I swallowed hard to again push down my anger. It was time for her to tell me what was going on.

"Thomas, the only reason I agreed to go to Abilene with my father was for us. I truly believed I could change his mind. You know how well that went. The best I was able to do was get him to acknowledge that there was nothing inherently abhorrent in the occupation of writing and—"

"How kind, but what does this have to do with Kennard?"

"Please, Thomas, let me tell this at my own pace. You've wanted to know what happened in Kansas, and it's time I told you everything. I kept this from you for so many reasons, but mostly I just couldn't find the words. This is very difficult."

I moved to the fireplace. I suddenly felt the need for something to hold on to.

"The day after we arrived in Abilene, Father was already busy with cattle trading or such, so he arranged for an escort to give me a tour of the town. I hadn't yet met my embroidery student so I couldn't write to you, and with

Father occupied there really wasn't anything else to do. When the wagon pulled up, Lowell was driving the team. I was so shocked I nearly collapsed. Father arranged it so Lowell was—"

Unsure if I had really heard her say Lowell Kennard was in Abilene, I waved my hands for her to stop. I needed a moment to clear away the wave of frantic thoughts. My hearing was sound. Mary went on to tell me Kennard was in Abilene the whole time she was there. I could hardly breathe.

At first Mary was so vexed she stayed in her room and refused to speak to either of them. Livid at Mary's disobedience, Mr. Harting instructed the innkeeper to lock Mary out of her room after breakfast. He demanded she attend to Kennard.

"Father and I quarreled until our voices were hoarse. I'd never seen him so beside himself. For that matter, I don't think I've ever been so upset in my life. After two days of carrying on like that, I finally agreed to the tour just so I could fix their flint."

It seems Lowell was very understanding of Mary's childish antics and patiently followed her for half a mile after she jumped out of the carriage and refused to get back in. He had knowledge of the area and seemed genuinely interested in making sure she knew her way around. Over the weeks, Mary found him polite and extremely attentive. He even arranged delivery of fresh blueberries each morning because he overheard her fondness for them.

To my credit, Henry, I did not say any of what raged through my head—at least not yet.

"Father knew I would seize any moment alone to talk about you, so Lowell usually joined us for dinner. After dinner Lowell and Father ushered me into the guest parlor to read or stitch so they could talk endlessly about business. As often as was believable I had a headache so I could return directly to my room. This was when I would read your letters, Thomas, and imagine our reunion. I wanted to go home, begged my father to let me return to New York, but he wouldn't escort me and forbade me to travel alone.

"I should have written you about Lowell, but how could I? I was trapped in Abilene and you were so involved with your work. There was nothing either of us could do. Then I wanted to tell you last week, but we've seen so little of each other that I didn't want to spoil our time together. Thomas, I've been so overwhelmed. I didn't know what to do."

When I remained silent, she went on to share how Lowell made a habit of complimenting her and leaving small gifts at her door. Even so, Mary remained adamant that they hardly knew each other well enough for him to propose. She believes the only reason he did was because he worried she might leave. He was right. Mary left for Newport the very next morning after his proposal. It turns out, she snuck away. Though she wanted to tell her father about her arrangement to visit me, she could not stand up to him. She left without saying a word to anyone.

"It doesn't matter anyway," she said. "Once I got here, I wrote Mother so she wouldn't worry. I begged her not to tell Father where I was, but he's begun writing me here too. I didn't tell him you were here, Thomas, but he knows of Lowell's proposal and demands I marry him."

Mary came up behind me and put her hand on my shoulder. I jerked away. She dropped her hand and said, "That's what happened in Abilene. That's all of it."

My grip on the fireplace mantle was so tight my

fingertips were numb. I did not trust myself to look at Mary, but there was still one unanswered question. I turned and faced her. My voice was thin.

"That isn't all of it, Mary. What did you say to the Muskrat when he proposed?"

She claims he would not let her give him an answer. He said something cryptic about her future and implored she speak with her father before giving her reply.

"And have you considered his proposal?" I asked.

Her eyes widened. "Of course not. How could you even think that?"

I strode to the window to move away from her astonished gaze and glanced through the parted curtains. Dark clouds tightened ranks.

"Thomas, I didn't think Lowell would continue with all of this after I left. I suppose I liked the attention but I never gave him any encouragement. Any thoughts of love are purely in his imagination," she said.

"So those pages of homely, slanted scrawl are filled with words of love?"

She rubbed her forehead. "No, that's not what I'm trying to say. Thomas, you have to understand that I wanted to protect you. You were all alone, lonely, and made it very clear you didn't even want to hear of dinner parties. How could I tell you something like this?"

My pulse raced. "Don't twist my words. I told you I didn't enjoy hearing of your escapades. I never said you should cavort with other men and then lie about it. You should have told me, Mary." I thought of all my letters. "I even wrote how wonderful it was you didn't have to spend time with the Muskrat. Oh, wait, excuse my insensitivity, Mr. Kennard, or should I just call him Lowell?"

Anger pressed against my chest. For weeks I had

endured the desperate uncertainty of our future and thwarted threats against my life while she enjoyed pleasant evenings with another man. Beads of sweat gathered at my temples as I met her stare.

"When you barely wrote full sentences from Abilene, Mary, I worried for your safety and that you were desperately lonely. As you continued to stay aloof, I thought maybe I was pushing too hard and felt guilty. Then I was elated when you said you wanted me in your life no matter the repercussions, but now I understand. I'm a fool. You were appeasing me. You've just been busy with an attentive suitor and didn't want me to know about it. Why bother telling me about secluded buggy rides or lavish gifts," I said, pausing to catch my breath. "Or the trivial matter of a blooming marriage proposal!"

"Thomas, keep your voice down. You don't want her to overhear us."

"That's what you're concerned with; that Abigail will hear me? Let her. Doesn't she already know all about Mr. Kennard? She seemed so excited by his letter. Surely you girls have chatted about the gent who brought you fresh blueberries every morning."

Mary slapped her hands on her hips, fury blazing in her eyes. "I haven't discussed anything with that woman. Do you think I'm brainless?"

"No, I think you're a liar. I think you didn't write because you were enjoying the Muskrat's attentions. Why not? He's an established businessman who holds charity balls and impresses your father. It's all very simple. You haven't said no to Kennard because you're considering his proposal."

"That's not so and you know it. You're not listening with your ears; you're listening with your oversized ego," she shouted. "As soon as you began your book you thought of me only when I didn't get in the way of your precious work. I came to this vacant mud bog to see you, but you've been 'carried away.' You weren't too busy to dine with the glamorous opera singer, were you Thomas? I saw the news clipping. Katya Petrova is stunning and you say you hardly noticed her. You're the liar."

I slammed my palm against the window frame. "Well that just beats the Dutch. After what you confessed you have the nerve to accuse me. And what would it matter if I were attracted to a beautiful opera singer anyway? You're soon to be Mrs. Mary Muskrat."

"I," she gasped for air, the halted sound shook against her chest and tears ran down her red cheeks. "I don't want to marry him, but he's the only one who's asked."

Her words felt like a blade through my stomach. For a moment the light dimmed. I turned and enunciated each word for fear of what I might say in haste. I was surprised to hear my voice shudder from rage. "You wanted me to wait for your father's blessing, so—"

"You deserted me to write some silly, adolescent novel."

I was so stunned I fell backward against the wall. Had I been farther away from the pine panels I would have fallen all the way to the floor.

"Thomas, I didn't mean . . . I'm so frustrated and—"

I raised my hand. "No. No. I understand. You're correct; I live in a world of make believe, a fantasy land, and I'm probably just another gadabout wasting time and my father's money with my silly novels."

I started toward the door.

"Thomas, wait, I didn't—"

"Wait for what?" I asked. When Mary said she wanted to build a life with me, I believed her. When she decreed she was going to Abilene, I apologized for trying to stop her and prayed for her safety. Then when I heard little from her for weeks, I feared she was tormented by the complexity of our affair. Instead I find out she was well occupied with escorts and marriage proposals and continues to go to great lengths to hide me and our attachment. How could I have been such a simpleton? Everything was clear.

"You're concerned with what ladies like Mrs. Winchester will think of you and your imprudent choice. If I were as famous as Henry you might reconsider, but Mr. Kennard's a satisfactory match and it's easier to obey your father. I was a frivolous summer novelty, but I'm sure any feelings you have for me will fade away quickly enough. And, of course, there's Mr. Kennard's considerable wealth and standing. He's a reputable figure not a stumbling scribbler. It seems you have what you really want, so I'll step aside. At least this writer of juvenile drivel is still a gentleman."

"You believe I have what I want? You think me capable of trifling with you, any man, for folly then marrying for wealth? What kind of man are you, Thomas Gadwell? You believe stepping aside and questioning my intentions makes you a gentleman?"

"I think that, Miss Harting, depends on the lady."

I left; Mary did not stop me.

The person who knocked on my door yesterday was Abigail's messenger with a brief note. Mary returned to New York. Abigail is relieved there will be less tension in her house.

So, Henry, I guess we can abandon the wrangle of blooming love and return to chastising the decline of American values; sit for hours and ramble about the inefficiencies of the world without exerting any effort. It is what I do best.

Mary Harting will wed Lowell Kennard, and I shall finish my work with a heavy pen and wiser perspective. Love is indeed a madness that ruins us all.

Your foolish,
Thomas

May 11, 1889.

DEAR MOTHER—

Happy Anniversary. By the time you read this, Father shall have taken you to a fine restaurant and given you a dazzling necklace. He has fine taste in jewelry and women.

Yesterday the sun at last graced the island, and though I fled the study for a refreshing stroll by the docks, I found a bitter outlook. The fishermen have returned. The air smelled of brine, chum, wet burlap, unfinished ale, dirty coats upon dirty men, and spilled oil. The putrid mixture means summer is near. And so is my deadline.

I must finish my work before crowds clutter the beaches with flying horseshoes. If I continue at my current pace and rigid routine, I hope to just make it. Therefore, Mother, for the time being I must insist we dispense with this unpleasant topic.

Indeed something happened with my young lady, and our brief union ended in the way of all failed love. We spoke careless, regrettable words, though I believe those are truer than the words we practice. She has not attempted to contact me, nor have I her. Your son is again an eligible bachelor.

Perhaps when I return to Boston we can speak of love and relationships as you so desire. Right now I find it all tiresome, like a jigsaw puzzle without an edge. I must leave you knowing your instincts are intact and your son grows ever wiser. If it helps to know I am not without prospect, another young lady fancies my company. Maybe I am as charming as you claim—and I thought it just maternal pride.

Your son,
Thomas

May 12, 1889.

BEAUREGARD—

How wonderful to hear from a man who begins his letter with an expletive on obliging native girls and then inquires of my state. You are redeemed only by your invitation.

My first inclination was to seek out my trunks. This was magnified when I stepped outside for the post and was pelted by a spring downpour before slipping and tearing open the elbow of my shirt, not to mention the skin beneath. As I still want to speak with you and will soon need a vacation, I shall mull over your offer. There is something we need to discuss about our time in Italy.

By the way, what does one pack to frolic on a yacht in the Mediterranean?

Thomas

May 12, 1889.

AVERY—

Final edits are enclosed and I am now focused on the polished draft of the next book. I have no intention of missing the June deadline.

T. G.

May 19, 1889.

DEAR MARY—

This letter may never see an envelope. Given my current state it may fuel the fire before I finish. Why then do I make overtures I will not fulfill? I must release my emotions at least on paper or wake one morning, put on my overcoat and heavy hunting boots, and walk into the sea until the world is again peaceful.

It has been over a month since our parting, yet when I stop writing and sit in the quiet for even a moment I am haunted by images of you and the Muskrat taunting my foolishness as you plan your happy future together. By now you may be living as newlyweds, setting up your household and waking in each other's arms while I nibble crackers and sleep just a few hours each night.

There are so many regrets forever trapped in Abigail's salon. If I could go back in time, I would change so much of what I said and how I reacted. I was caught off guard, and my anger flared more readily then I ever thought possible. But even so, I am still unable to reconcile your secrets with the forthright woman who so dazzled me in our seaside gazebo. Worse yet, I loathe myself for not proposing when I wanted. If I had, mine would have been your first. Instead you forever share that precious memory with someone else. Nothing can change that now.

And how could we let that meddling old shrew ruin our time together? I do believe her regard for me has changed. Mrs. Winchester seemed shocked by the tongue-lashing I gave her at the market. Perhaps I should have had better hold of my temper, but she chose a most fragile moment to confide her designs I marry her little protégé. She had the audacity to speak to me as a loving grandmother safeguarding my interests. My only regret is I must find a new grocer.

Mary, our spiteful words have not changed my feelings for you though I pray for such a release. My torment continues because I still love you. I love you. I have run out of fancy words for my affection and metaphors for your smile. But will I ever know your true feelings for me and my work?

Our fight could have ended with soft apologies had you refrained from attacking my Achilles heel. My pride, my oversized ego is too bruised. I wait for an apology but there is no letter in the box or telegraph at the office. I yearn to leave the image of your face here to gather mildew with the trinkets on the shelf and flee to a yacht in the sunshine. You were the woman to whom I pledged my heart, the mother of my children, the love that inspires writers to . . .

May 20, 1889.

DEAR MISS PETROVA—

Thank you for another generous invitation. I can think of nothing more intriguing than hearing you sing; however, a trip to Chicago is not any more plausible than San Francisco. Your tour sounds flawless, and I hope you are delighting in the fruits of your labor. Though unsure how long I will remain in Newport, I shall keep your schedule on my desk in hopes I may someday see you perform.

I wish you continued success.

Thomas M. Gadwell

May 24, 1889.
HENRY—
I thought you had traded Faneuil Hall for scones with the Queen. Welcome home.

As you have been submerged in the repressive ways of our forbearers, I take no offense. You are welcome here any time and never need wait for an invitation. I look forward to a visit. We can make considerable use of the wine cellar and immerse ourselves in the trade. If your stay includes any consolations other than my literary inadequacies, I ask that you remain in Boston until the spasm passes. My sights are stationed forward.

It might humor you to know that after Mary left Newport, Mr. Everett sent the missing arrest information on Lowell Kennard. He caught me at a most unfortunate time. I replied with a rather frenzied tirade on his tardiness and the societal lethargy that leads to economic devastation and men wearing open-necked shirts. The report itself did nothing to sweeten my mood.

The Muskrat was arrested for stealing a pipe and tin of tobacco. He was released to Mr. Harting, who I assume paid to have the record sealed. Of course Mr. Harting should prefer a petty thief for his daughter. Also, Mr. Everett still can not find any records on Lowell Kennard prior to his employment at Harting Railways in '79. Perhaps he did, in fact, appear as a ghost. I know I feel haunted.

Never mind, I am no longer worried about marauders and the Harting family. Life offers more productive endeavors like a visit from an old friend and finishing my draft on time.

See you soon,
Thomas

June 5, 1889.

DEAR MOTHER AND FATHER—

My delay in returning home is not from the interruption of interesting company or fine weather, as there has been little of either. My continued confinement is self-imposed and most critical.

With great humility I write to beg your permission to stay in Newport a bit longer. I know the summer home is soon full and apologize for the inconvenience. You know I would never ask for such a grand concession with so little notice unless the situation imperative. My deadline is fast approaching. I must and will meet my deadline. Regardless of the sacrifice, I shall not fail Avery or myself.

Your grateful son,
Thomas

WESTERN UNION TELEGRAM
Newport Island Office

JUNE 8 1889
URGENT TELEGRAM RECEIVED. MY SHIP SAILS TONIGHT.

SUMMER 1889

June 10, 1889.

TO MR. LOWELL KENNARD—

Your shameful display at the hospital this afternoon supports your reputation. That you were shocked by the circumstances does not explain your abhorrent behavior. As I wish to stifle any more unpleasantness, I request we meet this evening at the New York Polo Club. If you can employ civilized manners, we shall discuss our differences like gentlemen. If this is beyond your capacity, quite possible based on your colorful use of vulgar language, we shall reach a settlement in a more direct manner.

Thomas Marcus Gadwell

June 11, 1889.

MY DEAREST MARY—

Last evening I met with Mr. Kennard, and he is not the man he claims. I know this sounds ludicrous, but I must speak to my father at once. I leave New York for Boston in an hour.

My darling, this is urgent or I would never leave your hospital bed. Rest well and listen to the nurses. I shall return as soon as possible with what I hope are the answers to all our questions. If my theory about Lowell Kennard is correct, your father will never again insist you marry him.

With love,
Thomas

June 14, 1889.
DEAR HENRY—
Have you ever been amazed by how much can change in just a few days? This letter is meant as a chronicle of events, but as it is fantastic, you must read it straightaway. By the way, if you seek my company in Newport you will find only crusty bread and an even crustier caretaker.

As you may have read in the news, New York is still reeling after last week's horrendous riot. Wall Street has reopened even though ladies still slip on soot from the burned buildings and some men have taken to carrying pistols in their breast pockets. I applaud the honest Irishmen who took to the streets to protest oppression, but the battle against the corrupt union was indeed bloody. It was reported thirty-five men were slain and another fifty-five were wounded. The count, however, did not include the injuries of a young lady on her way home from teaching English.

My sweet Mary found herself trapped in the rampage for almost an hour before she was rescued by her student. With a broken ankle and deep cuts across his face and arms, Mr. Tzukernik carried Mary to safety. My gratitude is overwhelming; I just wish he had arrived sooner. I have yet to comprehend the terror she must have felt.

Miss Ross sent a telegram stating Mary was in the hospital, but the inept girl gave no indication of her condition. You can never imagine the horrors I conjured on my way to New York. For the first time in my life I was seasick. Then my arrival at the hospital caused a ruckus.

Mr. Harting was seated in the waiting room with Mary's older sister, her husband, and their new son. Before I could inquire of Mary's condition, Mr. Harting seized my arm and told the hospital staff I was involved in the riot. A nurse sent for the police while two orderlies held me down in a chair.

I gave the policeman my steamer ticket as alibi, but when Mr. Harting mentioned his personal friendship with the police chief, the officer pinned my hands behind my back and reached for his ruffles. It was a Harting of equal influence who rescued me.

Mr. and Mrs. Harting argued before Mr. Harting left in a rage. When I approached to thank Mrs. Harting, she demanded my silence, dragged me by the forearm to a seat in the corner of the lobby, and insisted we speak before she would allow me to see Mary.

Mrs. Harting recounted that when Mary returned from Newport she would not consider visitors and locked herself in her room. She refused to dress for dinner and could be heard crying through the bedroom door for hours on end. "That was your doing, I'm sure," she said.

I tried to apologize but she waved her index finger to stop me. "There's no need to apologize to me. I understand all too well, I assure you. I have two daughters." She lifted her handbag, fluffed the lace detailing on her skirt, then reset the bag on her lap before she continued.

"Mary wasn't eating much. She had no color at all. I tried to talk to her, but she's as stubborn as her father. Well, I couldn't let her continue that way, could I? She wasn't taking any air at all. I made her go. She didn't want to leave the house, but . . ." Mrs. Harting brushed a nonexistent hair from her cheek. "I made her go and tutor that horrible family. I just wanted her to enjoy an airing."

With a gloved hand she tugged down the edge of her black bolero jacket. "After the attack, Mary begged me to write to you. She wasn't sure you'd ever want to see her again, but I knew you'd come. Men always show up at the last moment." She examined me as if I were a prospective end table and sighed. "I knew Charlton's shenanigans would only make matters worse. He's never understood girls. I kept telling him . . . well that doesn't matter now. There's nothing to be done with girls in love. I should know." She stood and said, "Go and see Mary. And steady yourself, young man, she needs you."

She walked away before I could ask, but I suspect Mrs. Harting instructed Miss Ross to send the telegram.

Once I found Mary's room I paused in the hallway to do as Mrs. Harting suggested, but Henry, nothing could have prepared me. When I opened the door, my knees buckled.

The deep olive walls and walnut floor were a stark contrast to the crisp white linens covering Mary's puny frame. She was sleeping, breathing as if napping on a summer's afternoon, but her forehead was bandaged with thick gauze and her left arm was set in a sling. When I stepped closer, I saw her lips were swollen and cracked, cut marks covered her neck, and a deep purple bruise ran the length of her right cheek. The doctor told me her physical injuries will heal; however, Mary is so idealistic. I fear more than her arm broke that afternoon.

I have not cried since crushing my finger at summer camp, but right then I fell to my knees at her bedside and wept. My eyes were still closed when I felt Mary brush the tears from my cheek. I opened my eyes to find her looking at me with a tender smile. I took her hands and kissed the scratches on her palm and fingers. She never looked more radiant.

"Thomas," she whispered. Fresh tears ran down the side of her face and onto her pillow.

I pulled her hand to my heart. "Mary, can you ever

forgive me? I was a complete and utter imbecile. You were right about everything, my ego and my pride. I acted like a loon because I was jealous and afraid of losing you. Mary, I love you. I've loved you from the moment we danced under the stars at the hotel. When I learned you were hurt . . ." I was unable to continue.

Her voice was small but clear. "I love you too, Thomas."

She looked as if she wanted to say more but was too weak. Mary turned toward the sunlight streaming in from the window over her bed and I watched her body sink into the mattress.

I was still on my knees and what came next was so simple; so unlike my usual style of fumbling over too many words. "Will you marry me?" I blurted. Henry, you are the first to know we are engaged.

Mary never agreed to wed Kennard. Mary's sister, however, told me Mr. Harting accepted Kennard's proposal on Mary's behalf and has begun planning their wedding. It gives me chills to think my arrogance and her father's chicanery might have forced her to marry that swine. This brings me to what I must tell you, Henry. Mr. Kennard is a fraud.

Kennard had the unfortunate shock of walking into Mary's room just as we sealed our engagement with a kiss. He was flabbergasted, expressed his disgust in ruffian terms, and knocked over a tray of instruments as he stormed from the room. At my request, he agreed to meet with me that evening.

The Muskrat shook my hand like a long lost friend then bragged about the notable size of his real estate investments. This was distasteful and contrived to avoid the topic at hand. Sensing my disapproval, or perhaps realizing I was about to discuss the finality of his attachment to Mary, he began speaking of his childhood. I believe he was hoping to find common footing and felt my being from Boston, so near his home in Worcester, was the closest he would come. He had no idea how close.

Mr. Kennard told me he was a twin, though he lost his twin to smallpox. He and his brother loved to do acrobatics and once spent an entire summer building a fort on a lake. Have I ever told you of my childhood adventures? Henry, he was telling the story of my old friend William Crawley. That was *my* lake and *my* fort. I still have no idea how I stayed on the barstool. Of course he had no way of knowing my intimate knowledge of his tale. I let him foam at the mouth until his fabrication so exaggerated he stopped like a galloping horse before a pond.

He has stolen William's story as his own, and I must find out why. I have an idea, a sneaking suspicion of intrigue and malice. You see, along with his lies, I was also left with a terrible rash on my palm. How coincidence has played its hand—no less than a royal flush.

The train has just arrived in Boston so I must leave you wanting more. Seems you have taught me well.

Thomas

June 15, 1889.

MY PRECIOUS MARY—

I love you and hope you are healing with speed. I met with my father and unearthed gold. My prospecting now takes me to Worcester where all, I hope, shall be revealed. Our future depends on it.

Your adoring,
Thomas

June 19, 1889.

HENRY—

The treachery of deceit appeals to the wicked in ways honest men can never fathom. If I understood such altered minds I too would be tempted by money and command, but such ways are best left as stories to liven parties and debate over cigars. Sins unravel until the dishonest are left naked and shivering.

When last I wrote I had just arrived in Boston, rather late, and my parents were asleep. The quandary to wake my father lasted a full ten minutes, to which reason prevailed. I had a fretful night and was dressed and waiting for my father in the front hallway early the next morning.

Mother rose first. Fearing I was a thief, she threw a pewter candlestick at my head from the upstairs landing. My fortune was her awful aim. The candlestick knocked over a flower vase before making a pronounced chip in the marble floor. In response I glanced at the broken vase then asked if Father was awake. She shook her head and demanded we all eat breakfast before the inquisition.

It was not until I pushed cold eggs around my plate that Mother noticed my hand. She had seen that rash before and wanted to know why in the world I had handled talc.

"I haven't," I said. I eyed my father.

My mother huffed as she picked up our plates. "You're both giving me a rash. Go talk already, get it over with. I'm going to make some bread."

Father and I went into his study, but before he could take his usual debate position I said, "I know you wrote to me about it, but I need you to go through your dealings with William Crawley one more time."

He leaned against the corner of his desk with the dejected look of a felon awaiting sentencing. He said again he was not proud of what happened and saw no reason to dredge up the past. But his feeble protest did not crack my resolve. I told him it was time I knew all the details.

"Are you going to tell me why you're so interested or perhaps you want me to guess?" he asked. "From the look on your face, I agree with your mother. This has to do with a woman, not an old friend."

"Please, Father, you already admitted a great deal in your letter. I just have a few more questions then I'll never bring it up again. It'll be like the bribes that went in Boss Tweed's pocket."

He grumbled his consent then opened his humidor and shoved a cigar in his mouth. I took my place by the window but was too nervous to lean on the sill.

"I ran into William in '79 when I went to New York City to look into vacant land investments," Father said. "William was unshaven and had on a dirty overcoat. I started to walk away because he looked like an absurd soaplock. That's when he grabbed my arm and told me he worked as a bank teller at the Midland Bank in Worcester and found himself mixed up in the bank robbery."

I knew all of this, so I stopped him. I wanted to know more about the counterfeiting. Why did William agree to hold the counterfeiting plates instead of going to the police? Father told me William admitted wanting the bribe money to impress a girl. My father then looked at me hard. "He was acting like all stupid boys in love." When I ignored his comment, he added, "I think William was hornswoggled by—"

"Hornswoggled?"

"Don't be smart with me, Thomas. I think he was tricked into holding the counterfeiter's plates. The plates were evidence that would have convicted William and not the real shofulman. When William ran into me, federal agents wanted to question him."

I shook my head. The pieces did not fall into place. If William was in so much danger, why had he risked taking the plates to New York? He could have disposed of them in Worcester. My father looked a little troubled. He never thought to ask William that question.

I then asked my father if William had the counterfeit plates with him when they bumped into each other. No. William left everything at his hotel.

"Did you go to the hotel with William to get the plates?" I asked.

My father bit down on his cigar. "You're trying my patience, Thomas. You already know I destroyed the counterfeiting plates to protect your friend. What difference does it make where he gave them to me?"

I ignored his tone and instead asked if he ever met the other man, the counterfeiter, or if William mentioned his name. Though my father said he never met the counterfeiter, he told me his name was Irwin Bennett. I asked if he was certain.

"Of course I'm sure. Bennett was the man shot during the robbery. It was in the papers. You must remember his name."

My memory was dull but I admitted nothing. "Where was he shot?" I asked.

"In the vault."

"No, I mean where on his body?"

"Then be succinct. You know how much I hate . . ." He paused and commented I looked pale. Then he plucked the cigar from his mouth, stroked his mustache, and began tapping his foot. "So, did you ask her to marry you?"

If not for the shock, I could have acted ignorant and

plead he return to my questions. His bluntness astonished me, and so I simply answered yes.

"And what did she say?" He spoke with more excitement than I expected.

"She said she couldn't possibly say yes until she met my father to see if I'll be handsome in my old age. I'm afraid it's a tough call."

My father raised his eyebrows, tossed his cigar on his desk, and howled. His merriment was contagious and we laughed in waving fits. As Father leaned forward clenching his stomach, Mother burst into the room wielding a rolling pin.

"Want to try for my head again?" I asked between gasps of air.

We laughed even harder. Father fell into his chair. For several seconds Mother stood silent in the doorway looking back and forth between us. Then she dropped her rolling pin, rushed across the room, and flung her arms around my neck.

"Thank goodness," she whispered into my shoulder. "I thought you two were finally killing each other."

After a few minutes, Father cleared his throat and instructed me to share the news with Mother. When I told her of the engagement, she again flung her arms around me. She left us with an open bottle of champagne before rushing off to my aunt's house to write letters. Father then finished answering the rest of my questions. The next morning, I went straight to Worcester.

The Worcester County Hall of Records is well organized; however, just last year the archives were damaged by an arson fire. My quick trip turned into a grimy excavation through boxes of charred paper, and I spent the first day choking from fumes and ruining my white dress shirt. It was not until late into the second day my law internship was put to good use.

After five hours of sorting and restacking documents by type and year, I felt queasy and ready to forget my hunch about the counterfeiter, Mr. Bennett. If not for the rat that charged across a tall stack, I might have missed my Rosetta Stone. I picked up the file folder and blew sooty paw prints from the cover. It read, "Department of the Treasury, Worcester, 1879."

At last the plot has untwisted. This story involves a bank robbery, a wounded man, my father's unwitting aide to a counterfeiter, and the acts of fate no man can escape. Did you know talc is used to dry wet ink?

Sorry, Henry, but I must leave you here. The carriage is here to take me to Mr. Harting. You see, we have a rather urgent matter at hand. I shall give him his choice of swords or pistols.

Thomas

June 20, 1889.

MY FIANCEE—

If I were a great poet, or even a bad one mayhap, I would create a passionate piece about the inequities of a world ruled by those lusting after tangibles Solomon knew were nothingness. Then I would plunge a metaphoric sword into my chest. Alas, I am not a poet. You must put aside what your heart wants to believe and hear what I have to tell you. Open your heart and mind, my love, and hear me well.

As you took your first sure-footed steps in the hospital, I called on your father in his office. No man could claim a stronger, more sure gait as I strode down the long paneled corridor to his suite. Had I a shield of iron I would have cast it aside. My protection was truth.

Your father sat behind his impressive Henry II writing desk and appeared to be looking at the curio cabinet filled with model trains and antique shaving mugs. I startled him, but he regained his composure and stared at me in the doorway. It would have been an expensive evening at his poker table.

"What are you doing here, Thomas?" he asked.

It was a purposeful slight, addressing me by my first name as he would his stable boy, and it was designed to tilt my balance. My stance remained firm.

I motioned toward the leather tub chairs across from his desk. My manner was chipper as I expressed a compliment of the lovely day and offered I had good news to share with him. Your father agreed to my taking a seat but told me to get to my business or leave. He was in no mood for folly.

Though I too wanted to get to business, I waited a moment. My dear, I was a boy before an exam. In my rush to see your father, in my arrogant confidence, I forgot to plan my presentation.

"I would like to talk to you about Mr. Kennard, sir. I have information I think you'll find most enlightening."

He shifted forward in his chair.

"I shall say it bluntly, sir, as it's clear you don't temper your medicine with sugar. Mr. Kennard is a thief, a forger, and a liar. He is repugnant and shall soon be locked in prison."

If you are now confused, my darling, please continue. What I reveal is the truth. It seems our lives were intertwined long before we collided in the ballroom at the hotel. Fate has intervened on our behalf, and I am reminded how small the world sometimes seems.

"I sincerely hope you have evidence to support such slanderous remarks, Thomas," your father said. "Mr. Kennard has worked for me for nearly ten years and must marry my youngest daughter."

I found this an odd way to state what in fact was not so, but I pushed aside my urge to correct him and shared that on March 15, 1879, the Worcester Midland Bank was robbed. He interrupted, wanting to know if I thought Kennard was a bank robber.

"No. I'm afraid it's much worse. May I go on?"

He nodded but was silent.

I next explained how the thieves were caught and the case appeared solved. There was just one slight problem. The amount of money recovered by the police did not match the amount taken. Your father huffed and asked why he should care if thieves spent some of their ill-gotten gains. It was a sound conclusion; however, they were not short of funds. I explained the bags contained too much currency.

"Counterfeits," he murmured.

I was inspired by your father's quick intelligence and continued with carriage.

The extra bills were indeed counterfeit. And because the money was stolen directly from the bank vault, the Treasury Department needed to find out how the counterfeits got into bank funds. There was either an unobservant employee or a criminal on the bank's payroll. The tellers were questioned and managers submitted detailed staff reports. Some of the reports were very entertaining. When I then told your father one of the tellers was fired for handing out extra cash to pretty girls, he replied, "You're inventing this."

"On the contrary, the Worcester records sizzled with information."

During my research, I also found information about an assistant manager, Irwin Bennett. Mr. Bennett was one of three managers entrusted with keys to the bank vault. Naturally he was a suspect; however, he was never questioned by the Treasury. Just a few weeks after the robbery, he quit his post and moved without notice.

I paused with this revelation, anticipating your father's question, but he was stoic. So I further explained.

Mr. Bennett was never questioned because he was considered a hero. The robbery took place at two o'clock, the exact time when Mr. Bennett opened the vault. Unsuspecting Mr. Bennett was trapped alone with the gunmen. The specifics are unknown, as Mr. Bennett was never interviewed, but the investigators assumed Mr. Bennett attempted to thwart the robbery.

With this, your father wanted to know why the treasury investigators made such an assumption.

"Because he was shot," I said.

"What in the world does this have to do with Mr. Kennard? Get to your point."

Ignoring his demand, I asked if he knew about my exchange with Kennard at the hospital. He had heard all about the incident (I must assume from Kennard himself), and called it disgraceful. I agreed it was a paltry display and shared with your father how Kennard and I met that evening to discuss the situation.

"Mr. Kennard shared a most interesting story of his childhood. The particulars are unnecessary, but I must implore you to believe the story he shared was not his own. Coincidence is startling sometimes. The elaborate details of his childhood were that of an old friend of mine, a Mr. William Crawley," I said.

Your father broke in and told me to start making sense or get out of his office. He did not care or see any reason why Kennard would make up a trivial childhood story.

"Not made up, sir, we'll say it was borrowed. And why of course is the question. It's apparent Mr. Kennard knows my friend, William Crawley, and in 1879, the year of the robbery, Mr. Crawley was a bank teller at Worcester Midland Bank."

Your father turned in his chair; his mysterious expression replaced with flaring nostrils and flushed cheeks. "Gadwell, you're talking in circles. I retain my initial judgment that you're a half-wit and I'll see to it—"

This time I stopped him and launched into the details. "The bank manager, Mr. Bennett, and my friend Mr. Crawley were printing the counterfeit money. I know this for a fact, just as I know I love your daughter. On the day of the robbery, Mr. Bennett was in the vault switching the bills when he was interrupted before he had time to withdraw the real currency. Bennett must have known if the money was recovered the counterfeits would be discovered. I believe he was shot while trying to recover the fake bills."

Your father stood up and paced in front of the window. "So Bennett and Crawley printed snide bills? I have no interest in these men. I've never heard of either of them."

But he has, my dear, and so have you. You see, Mr. Bennett did not die from the gunshot wound but was badly injured. He was shot in the right cheek. Reportedly it was a deep wound that would leave a remarkable scar.

Color drained from your father's face, but I then said what he needed to hear. "Mr. Bennett, the man involved in counterfeiting, extortion, and theft is without a doubt your Mr. Kennard. And I believe Mr. Kennard is still printing counterfeits."

My dearest, I hope learning the truth about Kennard is not too great a shock.

I thought I was prepared for any reaction; he might not believe me or demand more evidence. I even imagined a sincere pat on the shoulder for saving his daughter from such a man. It is fair to say I was flabbergasted when he began laughing.

He laughed in deep, powerful bursts that would have been infectious if I were not the cause. When at last he caught his breath he turned and stared at me. I reaffirmed the validity of my information and made clear my true regard and concern for his whole family. He cracked his knuckles then said, "I underestimated you, Thomas. You're slick. To think I let you continue with such lunacy—"

"I assure you—"

He pounded his fists on the desk. "You can assure me of nothing, you arrogant ne'er-do-well. Do you think I'm an idiot? I'm no fool. I know all about your letters to Mary. I thought my man would scare you off. Unfortunate outing for carriage problems, but you had fair warning. Of course I had to pull my man when Mary ran off. I couldn't risk her getting hurt."

When we are again in each other's arms I will explain in delicate terms a most indelicate incident.

He leaned across his desk. "You've paraded your insubordination for months, and now you want me to believe riddles as if I were one of those Nancy-boy editors I see prancing down Madison Avenue. What I believe is that you're a scoundrel who would say or do anything to win Mary.

"And where is your proof?" he asked. "You're accusing a loyal and trusted member of my company based on nothing more than a childhood story and old scar. I didn't build my business on speculation or the hearsay of men without sense. My wealth was made from the sweat and blood of loyal men who put in a hard day's labor—men like Lowell Kennard. You're just another—"

"That's enough!" I leapt to my feet and met his glare. "I've endured your insults and reproach because I love your daughter and know how much she wants your approval. But now you are accusing me of being underhanded while you defend a criminal and admit your attempt on my life. You're reprehensible. Money really doesn't care who owns it. You're not a gentleman, you're a fiend."

He shouted for me to get out of his office. "And if I find out Mary has any more contact with you, I'll toss her to the street like a washwoman."

Mary, I agonized if I should reveal all that was said by your father. I take nothing away from his rearing of such a wonderful woman, but if you are to have your own life you must live unrestrained by the perceptions of childhood.

I went to the door but stopped at the threshold and faced your father before leaving. "I shall present my information about Kennard to the authorities. More importantly, I'll hold nothing from the future Mrs. Gadwell. I have complete faith in Mary's competent judgment."

There is one important fact I kept from your father but tell you now in trust and confidence. I was able to link these facts together because my father helped William Crawley escape justice. I even disclose my father made a tidy sum. Who could predict his assistance would someday aid his own son's nemesis?

Though you longed for your father's approval and I wanted you to wed a famous author, it seems both are doubtful. You see, there is something else you should know. I missed my deadline. Putnam pulled my contract, as did Avery. Funny, but none of it matters anymore. I indeed have what I most desire.

My dearest, I shall wait as long as you need to adjust to what has transpired. Then we can marry in Boston and live as the fable ends. Am I too optimistic? Do I presume too much? Will you cast aside my findings as the illusions of a lunatic? I have undying faith in the future Mrs. Thomas Gadwell.

Ever yours,
Thomas

June 28, 1889.

MY FRIEND—

I left you like a prisoner swinging from a rope. If you were anyone but a man in love with the perfect story, I would apologize. Henry, are you ready for the denouement? Even with the outline and what I believed were all the elements for the baroque ending, what happened was far more fantastic. Mr. Harting and Lowell Kennard are far more dangerous than I suspected.

By now you have received my letter depicting my impetuous meeting with Mr. Harting. Upon reflection, I should have expected his reaction. He is so like my father, headstrong and convicted. Men like that loathe cracks in their foundation. I arrived with a sappy grin and large chisel. No wonder he was angry.

Mary believed everything I uncovered. She told her father she would never marry Kennard and officially announced our engagement. A few days later she was released from the hospital and returned home to make preparations for Boston. When she got home, however, Mary found her father waiting for her in the solarium. The rest of the family and servants were ordered out of the house. He demanded to speak with her alone.

Mary wrote their conversation word for word, as if she would never forget even one fantastic syllable. For brevity and clarity, I shall summarize. What I am about to reveal is copyrighted. Yes, my friend, this shall someday be a best-seller.

After I presented my case, Mr. Harting did in fact cross-hackle Mr. Kennard about his alternate identity and banking ventures. From Mr. Harting's account, Kennard was forthcoming.

Lowell Kennard, born Irwin Bennett in Worcester, Massachusetts, worked as a teller and taught at the evening banking school run by the Tenth National Bank. There he met my old pal William Crawley, and the pair began printing counterfeits. When Bennett was promoted to bank manager, the promotion quite literally opened the doors for their next venture.

After the bank robbery blunder, Bennett fled to New York to begin a new life using the assumed name Lowell Kennard. This explains why Mr. Everett was unable to find information on Kennard prior to 1879. To legitimize his new identity, Kennard needed reputable employment so he accepted a job as a bookkeeper with Harting Railways. He also began another printing project by cover of nightfall. I shall get to that in a moment.

By 1880, a series of rail accidents and labor strikes left Mr. Harting overextended and panicked. Stock prices were down, which meant a considerable risk to Mr. Harting's personal finances. In short, he was in jeopardy of losing everything. This was when Mr. Kennard approached Mr. Harting with a profitable scheme. According to his own admission, Mr. Harting never questioned Kennard's methods. Instead, Mr. Harting promoted Kennard.

Under Kennard's direction, Mr. Harting created a fictitious corporation, secured a large loan, and solicited help from his cousin living in London. Kennard was again partnered with Mr. Crawley (I have yet to decide if I shall share this unsettling news with my father), and the two designed a new counterfeiting press. With all the players at the table, the joint business venture began in the fall of '82; Mary was just fourteen.

Henry, do you recall the scandal you stumbled upon in London? Even as I commit this to paper, I am awed by such an elaborate international con. Mr. Harting, William

Crawley, and Lowell Kennard have been printing and selling counterfeit United States bonds. Having learned from the bank mishap, Kennard even set up a swindle to trade the counterfeit bonds for a legal commodity.

Mr. Harting's cousin in London locates foreign investors dabbling in U.S. cattle and farming. Mr. Harting and Kennard then offer generous amounts of phony American bonds in exchange for cattle and crops. Overjoyed by their windfall, the investors hold the counterfeit bonds until full maturity while Harting and Kennard sell the cattle and crops for real currency. Their success surpassed all expectations, and there seemed no end in sight. Then a year ago Kennard revealed a deep secret.

Kennard told Mr. Harting he was in love with Mary and wanted her as his wife. Outraged, Mr. Harting refused to even consider letting an unscrupulous charlatan marry his precious daughter. They argued; however, the feud had to wait until after the family vacation in California. This is where I stumbled in like a drunken actor who had forgotten his lines. While Mary and I frolicked, Mr. Harting dealt with harassing telegrams and letters from Kennard. The day before Mr. Harting dragged Mary back to New York, Mr. Kennard played his final hand.

Kennard revealed a second and more interesting set of business records that implicated Mr. Harting as the sole perpetrator of their illegitimate operation. Kennard had planned for his escape, except he no longer wished to flee. He wanted Mary, and the blackmail was straight-forward.

Mr. Harting first attempted to fabricate equally damaging documents about Kennard. Mary and I witnessed this covert exchange in San Diego. Unfortunately, Mr. Harting's would-be accomplice cheated him. Cornered and desperate, Mr. Harting invited Kennard to family dinners and galas hoping all would take a natural course. Mary, however, was preoccupied. You can see why Mr. Harting detested my very existence. He was on the verge of ruin while I wrote love letters.

When I burst into Mr. Harting's office with accusations of Kennard's nefarious endeavors at the bank, it was in fact the first he had heard of that caper. Mr. Harting was abusive in efforts to shake loose bona fide evidence against Kennard. My story, though interesting, has proved worthless. Kennard insists Mary accept his marriage proposal within twenty-four hours or he will go the police with the forged documents.

Charlton Harting fell to his knees, clutched Mary's skirt, and begged her to save the family fortune and reputation. He assured Mary of Kennard's true affections and offered an extraordinary allowance if she married him. For the first time in her life Mary refused her father. She is packed and we leave for Boston at the end of the week. I have never been so proud of anyone in my life.

So now you know the whole tale. Are you satisfied in the telling? Seems there was no shortcut on this trip, and I tripped on every rock in the road. Still, I believe I needed to take this path in order to learn a most valued lesson.

Writing is not the imitation of life; it is the exploration of living. Lift your head from the pages, my friend, and feel the sun on your face. The world awaits, and we have more to offer than a good story. Though my cheeks are burned and I know there are more rocks ahead, I have never been more content and have also answered all but one question.

Henry, will you be my best man?

Your friend,
Thomas

Summer 1888

September 15, 1888.
DEAR AVERY—
Before you top your threatening telegrams with a rabid dog, the novel is complete. If you are now pawing through your desk for a calendar, allow me to assist. By my calculations, I am a week early. Wonders never cease.

You should let Harpers know your relentless pestering inspired me and in fact found a place in this new book. Before you worry for your reputation, rest assured you are not the only one immortalized in these letters. It turns out my family and friends really are characters. I should warn I strayed from another adventure novel, but the idea to mingle intrigue and romance into my ordinary life was inspired.

Did I tell you it was Henry who convinced me writing amid the beauty of the Hotel Del Coronado would loosen my writer's block? He claimed the salty breeze would clear the dust between my ears. Henry could never have predicted the woman on the upstairs balcony dousing herself with talcum powder. Each morning began with a fresh dusting. Nevertheless, my writer's block was cured by my propensity for observation and the hotel's diverse activities. In fact, you would rather enjoy the gaming here, especially the hunting. All summer there was a contest to see who could bag the muskrat family freeloading under the gazebo.

Once this package is sealed, I sail for Greece to make amends with Beau and attend the International Magician's Training Symposium and Souvlaki Bake. Regrettably, I shall miss Harpers' extensive publicity meeting, but surely they would never squelch a man's lifelong dream of pulling coins from unsuspecting ears. By the by, if in my absence, you happen upon my father, flee before he shares his dissertation on how writers and agents are the embodiment of lethargy and an economic burden on proper society. He sends his regards.

Avery, I must leave you here to get to the post and bid a final farewell to my beautiful muse. As I mentioned, this epistolary novel was inspired, and who stirs men more than a lovely creature. You know I never even found out her name. Ours was a love created by the flawlessness of imagination. She was the woman of my dreams, and though we never met, she was delightful and perfect as I watched her from across the room.

Your friend always,
Thomas

ABOUT THE AUTHOR

Gina L. Mulligan is a veteran freelance journalist for numerous national magazines and the author of the award-winning novel, *Remember the Ladies.* After her own diagnosis, Gina founded Girls Love Mail, a charity that collects handwritten letters of encouragement for women with breast cancer. As a result of her charitable work, she's been featured on the nationally syndicated television talk show *The Steve Harvey Show* and on websites for *People* magazine and *TODAY*.

To learn more or request Gina as a speaker, go to www.GinaMulligan.com.